"*Marriage is a gamble, Laura.*

"Even for people who are madly in love, it's a risk."

"But they're at least starting out with something between them," she whispered.

"So are we." He put his hands on her shoulders, turning her to face him. The look in his eyes made her shiver.

Reflected there were all the memories she'd tried so hard to ignore. And if she'd thought he didn't want her, it was obvious that she was wrong. He was making no secret of his hunger. It was in his eyes, those clear green eyes that had haunted her dreams, that left her flushed and breathless when she woke.

"That's just . . . physical," she got out, trying to sound cool. Hoping he wouldn't release her, because she wasn't at all sure her knees would support her.

"Don't underestimate it. A lot of marriages are based on less. . . ."

Dear Reader,

Once again, we've rounded up a month of top-notch reading for you—just right for the hot weather! Heather Graham Pozzessere, a *New York Times* bestselling author, has penned our American Hero title, *Between Roc and a Hard Place*. This is the story of a not-quite-divorced couple who meet up again in a very... unique way. And once they do, boy! The sparks really start flying then—and you'll want to be there to catch all the action.

The rest of the month is pretty special, too. Marie Ferrarella returns with the second title in her series called "Those Sinclairs!" *Heroes Great and Small* is a fitting follow-up to last month's *Holding Out for a Hero*. And later in the year look for brother Nik's story in *Christmas Every Day*. Dallas Schulze makes a welcome return appearance in the line with *Secondhand Husband*, a tale of love growing—as I guess it always does—in strange and mysterious ways. Finish off your reading with Barbara Faith's *Cloud Man* (this hero makes an absolutely unforgettable entrance), Desire author Cathryn Clare's *Chasing Destiny* and new author Debbie Bryce's *Edge of Darkness*. As always, it's a lineup of books so good you'll want to read every one.

And in coming months, look for more great romantic reading here at Intimate Moments, with books by favorite authors like Naomi Horton, Justine Davis, Emilie Richards, Marilyn Pappano and Doreen Roberts, to name only a few. Join us!

Yours,

Leslie Wainger
Senior Editor and Editorial Coordinator

SECONDHAND
HUSBAND

Dallas
Schulze

Published by Silhouette Books New York
America's Publisher of Contemporary Romance

SILHOUETTE BOOKS
300 East 42nd St., New York, N.Y. 10017

SECONDHAND HUSBAND

Copyright © 1993 by Dallas Schulze

All rights reserved. Except for use in any review, the reproduction or utilization of this work in whole or in part in any form by any electronic, mechanical or other means, now known or hereafter invented, including xerography, photocopying and recording, or in any information storage or retrieval system, is forbidden without the permission of the publisher, Silhouette Books, 300 E. 42nd St., New York, N.Y. 10017

ISBN: 0-373-07500-6

First Silhouette Books printing June 1993

All the characters in this book have no existence outside the imagination of the author and have no relation whatsoever to anyone bearing the same name or names. They are not even distantly inspired by any individual known or unknown to the author, and all incidents are pure invention.

®: Trademark used under license and registered in the United States Patent and Trademark Office and in other countries.

Printed in the U.S.A.

DALLAS SCHULZE

loves books, old movies, her husband and her cat, not necessarily in that order. She's a sucker for a happy ending, and her writing has given her an outlet for her imagination. She hopes that readers have at least half as much fun with her books as she does! Dallas has more hobbies than there is space to list them, but is currently working on a doll collection.

Prologue

The sharp scent of floor wax and cleaning fluid overlay the duller, more powerful smell of fear and hope. In contrast to the antiseptic white hallways beyond the deep alcove, the decor was pale peach and warm coral. Paintings of happy children playing with brightly colored balloons decorated the walls. The waiting room on the obstetrics floor of the hospital in Denver, Colorado, reflected optimism and hope for the future, as was appropriate for a place where happy events were a daily event.

The room had only one occupant at the moment. He stood in front of a watercolor portrait of a mother and child, his pale green eyes focused on the happy picture without seeing it. Broad-shouldered, lean hipped and tall, he stood with his feet braced apart, his hands in his pockets.

Conner Fox looked like a man accustomed to being in control of himself and his surroundings. A crumpled hospital gown lay on the seat next to him, dull green against the nubbly coral cover. He'd stripped it off in those first terrible minutes after the nurses had rushed him from the delivery room, leaving him with the memory of Rachel lying pale against the delivery table, all the life drained from her, her strong features frighteningly empty.

It seemed aeons ago, but he knew it had been barely thirty minutes. He'd felt every minute crawl past, every second seeming an hour. It was three o'clock in the morning and the hospital was quiet around him.

Less than twenty-four hours ago, Rachel's labor pains had barely begun and she'd laughed at him when he insisted that they start for the hospital immediately. She'd wanted to have the baby at home, but Conner had flatly refused to even consider it. She was too precious to him to risk something going wrong when they were forty miles from the nearest doctor and nearly a hundred from a hospital.

"What could go wrong? Look at these hips." She'd patted her broad hips. "I'm built like a peasant woman. I'll be able to bale hay until the baby's born and then get up and clean out the stables."

"If I catch you near a bale of hay anytime in the next eight months, I'm going to tan your butt," he'd promised her.

"Ooo! Now the truth comes out. You're a wife beater." Her eyes had laughed up at him, golden brown and sparkling with life.

"Only when she deserves it," Conner had told her, his arms sliding around her waist to pull her close.

"You're having this baby in a hospital." Though the words were a command, he knew Rachel had given in because she heard the fear in his voice, not because she was afraid to cross him. He was putty in her hands, and she knew it.

So they'd started the drive to Denver the moment her labor pains had begun. And once they'd arrived at the hospital, he'd been with her every moment, coaching her on her breathing, trying not to let her see how much her pain frightened him.

Everything had gone just as it should until half an hour ago. Though he'd been focused on Rachel, he'd sensed the change in atmosphere. Suddenly there was a tension that hadn't been there before, a feeling of urgency in the low murmurs exchanged between doctor and nurse. He'd looked to where the doctor stood between Rachel's updrawn knees and seen the bright tint of blood staining the covers. Too much blood. His eyes had shot back to Rachel's face to find her eyes closed in weariness, her face the color of paraffin. His hand tightened over hers, but there was no response.

"What's wrong?" His tone was quiet but held demand.

"She's hemorrhaging." The doctor didn't look up but continued to work with a calm speed that conveyed more urgency than any dramatic statement could have.

"Rachel?" Conner's voice held equal parts demand and terror as he looked back at his wife. But there was no response. And then a nurse was taking Rachel's hand from his, urging him from the room.

"Please, Mr. Fox. We're doing everything we can for your wife."

Conner had let himself be pushed outside and then stood there staring at the blank door. Rachel was behind that door. His life was behind that door. He should be there with her. He put his hand on the door and then stopped. The last thing Rachel needed was for him to distract the medical staff. His hand dropped to his side, his fingers slowly curling into a fist.

Since then, there'd been nothing to do but wait. And then the waiting was over.

"Mr. Fox?"

Conner closed his eyes at the sound of the doctor's voice. He didn't want to turn, didn't want to see the look in the older man's eyes, didn't want to hear the words he knew were coming, the words he'd been expecting ever since they'd pushed him from the room, away from Rachel.

But there was nothing to do but turn, nowhere to look but into Dr. Richmond's exhausted, anguished eyes.

"She's dead." Conner's words were a statement, not a question.

"I'm sorry. We did everything we could. There was no indication of any problem before this." The doctor continued to talk, explaining what had happened, the hemorrhaging they hadn't been able to stop, but Conner was no longer listening.

The whys didn't matter. Nothing mattered except that Rachel was dead. He was never going to see her smile again, never going to hear her laugh, never going to hold her close in his arms, feeling her heart beat against his, feeling his world fall into place because she was with him.

"We were able to save the baby."

Conner blinked, dragging his thoughts back to the present. "The baby?" It took him a moment to understand what the doctor was saying.

"A girl. She's fine, Mr. Fox. Seven and a half pounds."

"A girl." Rachel had wanted a boy. She'd been so determined to give him a son, determined that they were going to start their own dynasty. All he'd wanted was for his wife and child to be safe and healthy. Looks like neither of them had gotten what they wanted, he thought bitterly.

"You can see your daughter if you'd like, Mr. Fox."

What he'd like was to see his wife, alive and smiling. But that wouldn't happen. Never again. Conner allowed the doctor to take his arm and lead him down the hallway. Not into the delivery room, he registered vaguely. Was Rachel still in there? No, there was no Rachel anymore. He couldn't seem to get his mind wrapped around the concept, couldn't seem to grasp the reality of her death.

When he stepped into the room, a nurse rose from a chair. Her eyes were overly bright, and it occurred to Conner that she looked as if she wanted to cry. Funny that this woman—this stranger—should want to shed tears for Rachel's death when he couldn't seem to feel anything at all. Nothing but a huge, aching emptiness in the pit of his stomach.

"She's a beautiful baby, Mr. Fox." The nurse's voice was soft, her middle-aged face anxious.

Conner's eyes dropped to the blanket-wrapped bundle in her arms as she stopped in front of him. She hesitated, her eyes cutting to the doctor's face when Conner made no move to take the baby from her. Dr.

Richmond shook his head slightly, telling her not to force the issue.

"Look. Healthy and beautiful." She eased the edge of the blanket back, and Conner saw his daughter for the first time. Her face was red, her eyes pale blue and unfocused. One tiny fist escaped the pastel blanket to wave in the air over her face.

Conner's expression didn't change. There was no light in the ice-green of his eyes. He didn't reach out to touch her, didn't offer his finger for her tiny hand to grasp. He only stared at her in silence, the skin over his cheekbones stretched taut and a muscle ticked along his jaw.

The silence stretched, broken only by the tiny grunting noises the baby made. Casting another anxious look at the doctor, the nurse lifted the bundled infant in her arms.

"Would you like to hold her, Mr. Fox?"

For a moment, it seemed as if he hadn't heard her, or if he had, that he wasn't going to respond. But then his eyes lifted slowly to her face and the cold emptiness there made her actually step back a pace.

"No. I don't want to hold her."

Without another word and without looking at his daughter again, Conner turned and walked out of the room. The door shut behind him with a whisper of sound.

"The look in his eyes," Nurse McKenzie murmured. "Like he didn't feel a thing looking at her." Her arms tightened protectively around the baby as if to shield her from the remembered chill of her father's gaze.

"He's just lost his wife," Dr. Richmond reminded her. "He'll need some time to adjust." He reached out to touch the infant's soft hand, smiling as her fingers closed over his, her grip strong. "You're a fine, beautiful little girl. You're just going to have to have some patience with your daddy."

His smile faded as he pulled his finger from her grasp. "It's time she went to the nursery," he said, weariness thick in his voice.

"Yes, Doctor. We'll take good care of you until your daddy comes back," she murmured to the baby as she left the room.

Dr. Richmond watched her leave and then shook his head, his shoulders slumping. God, what a night. He pinched two fingers over the bridge of his nose and squeezed his eyes shut, wondering if there wasn't something he could have done differently. He shook the thought away. Second-guessing himself wasn't going to bring Rachel Fox back.

Straightening his shoulders, he pushed open the door and stepped into the hall. Glancing to the left, he saw Nurse McKenzie carry the newborn down the hallway that led to the nursery. Poor little scrap. What a hell of a way to start her life, half orphaned and her father grieving.

Shaking his head, he turned in the other direction. He could only hope that Conner Fox wasn't going to blame his daughter for his wife's death. Grief could do funny things to people. He'd try to get Conner to join a support group when he returned to see his daughter. *If* he returned.

Chapter 1

Three years later

"I'm sorry, Mr. Fox, but I'm going, and that's all there is to it." Margaret Cuthbert's round face was set with determination, her small mouth firm.

"Mrs. Cuthbert, when I hired you, you understood the situation." Conner's whiskey-rough voice revealed his thinning patience. "I told you the ranch was isolated, and you said that wasn't a problem."

"There's isolation, Mr. Fox, and then there's solitary confinement," she informed him tartly. "I've been here six months, right through most of the winter. I endured nearly three weeks of being snowed in with no phone. And no one to talk to, I might add, since you saw fit to spend most of your time out of the house."

"There was stock to tend to. This is a working ranch, not a health spa."

"Be that as it may, a person needs a little stimulation or they just wither up and die."

Conner could have pointed out that she showed no signs of withering. Her stout frame had a comfortable amount of padding, more than enough to stave off any possibility of her wasting away. But he doubted it would be worth mentioning.

"What about the child?" he asked, making one last attempt to persuade her to change her mind. "She's grown fond of you. Are you just going to leave her?"

"Mary will adjust to a new nanny quite easily. Your daughter, Mr. Fox, is blessed with a sunny temperament and a fondness for people in general. Obviously, a trait inherited from her late mother," she added pointedly. Now that she was leaving, she saw no reason to conceal her opinion of her employer.

Conner's jaw tightened, more at the reference to Rachel than at the implied insult. Damn the woman, then. He'd had enough of her disapproving face to last him a lifetime.

"I assume you'll stay until I've had time to find a replacement?" he asked, foregoing any attempt to persuade her to stay.

"I'll stay for a little while, but as I told you, my daughter's baby is due in six weeks and I want to be there in plenty of time. I don't want to miss the birth of my first grandchild. It's such a special time." She smiled softly, apparently forgetting her cordial dislike of him in the pleasure of contemplating the blessed event.

"Is it?" Conner's eyes were icy with indifference, his voice a bored drawl. Mrs. Cuthbert's mouth tightened angrily, her round cheeks flushing with annoyance.

"What you need, Mr. Fox, is not another nanny, but a wife. Someone who has a reason to put up with your ill temper, as well as the isolated situation. Someone, perhaps, who has absolutely nothing to lose and would, therefore, find the life you can provide something of an improvement."

"Thank you for the suggestion, Mrs. Cuthbert. I'll keep it in mind." Conner had the satisfaction of seeing disappointment flicker in her pale eyes. If she'd been hoping that her outrageous words would spark an explosion, she was doomed to disappointment. It would take more than Mrs. Cuthbert's petty sniping to do that.

She stared at him for a moment, the wind knocked out of her sails by his calm response. After a moment, she muttered that he'd better not take too much time in finding a replacement and then turned and left, totally deflated.

Conner stared at the door she'd pulled shut behind her. After a while, he picked up the pack of cigarettes that lay on the desk. He'd quit smoking when they found out Rachel was pregnant, started again after Mary was born. The first nanny he'd hired had thrown a fit about the damage his smoking could do to an infant's lungs, so he rarely smoked in the house and then only in his office.

Drawing in a lungful of smoke, he contemplated Mrs. Cuthbert's announcement that she was leaving. That would make five nannies in the past three years. If the isolation didn't get to them, the winter did. Hiring someone to take care of the baby had been a necessity. He couldn't run a ranch and change diapers at the same time. He'd hoped to find someone willing to stay for a few years, to give the child the stability Rachel would have wanted for her.

Rachel.

Conner stubbed out the half-smoked cigarette and rose from the desk. Shoving his hands in his pockets, he went to stand in front of the window. The magnificent panorama of the Rocky Mountains spread out before him. Snow crept down their sides, a pale reminder that winter had only recently relinquished its claim to the lower elevations. It lingered close enough to strike again.

They'd had a snowstorm in May the first spring after he and Rachel had been married and she'd teased him about the weather in Colorado, asking if winter was the only season the state had. She'd been born and raised in Arizona. But she'd adapted to the winters as if born to them, coming to love the stark beauty of the snowcapped Rockies that loomed at the western end of the valley that held the ranch.

Conner blinked, forcing the memories away as he reached for the cigarettes he'd just put in his shirt pocket. Lighting one, he was aware that his fingers weren't quite steady.

What you need, Mr. Fox, is not another nanny, but a wife.

He'd had a wife. What he needed was someone to care for the daughter she'd died giving birth to. He narrowed his eyes against the smoke. There were some horses he wanted to look at in southern California. He'd planned on making the trip later in the year, but he could go now.

Gunner Larsen would be here in the next couple of days. He always showed up about now. He could leave Gun in charge of the ranch—one of a very small handful of men he'd trust to take care of things. Two weeks—three at most—and he could be back, maybe with a couple of new mares. And with someone to take Mrs. Cuthbert's place.

Surely, in a city the size of L.A., there had to be a woman who liked kids, one who wouldn't think that being without cable television was tantamount to Stone Age living. He could offer a decent salary and no living expenses. All he asked was that she'd care for one three-year-old child.

What you need, Mr. Fox, is not another nanny, but a wife. Someone who has a reason to put up with your ill temper, as well as the isolated situation. Someone, perhaps, who has absolutely nothing to lose and would, therefore, find the life you can provide something of an improvement.

Hearing the echo of Margaret Cuthbert's words, Conner turned and stubbed the cigarette out before reaching for his hat. Maybe she was right on the last part, anyway. Maybe he did need someone who had nothing to lose. And when he found her, he'd hire her—he sure as hell wasn't going to marry her.

Laura Halloran stared at her reflection in the mirror over the bar. Cigarette smoke made the image hazy and a little indistinct. Not that it mattered. She saw the same reflection in the mirror every evening when she was getting ready for work. A face that was neither pretty nor plain but fell into some never-never land between the two. Blue eyes—nice blue eyes—she thought with a touch of defiance. But their shape and color was lost under the weight of heavy blue eye shadow, black eyeliner and thick layers of mascara. Her mouth was just a mouth and her hair was an unremarkable brown, but it was thick and soft and had enough natural curl to give it body. All in all, nothing to write home about.

She sighed and slid one aching foot out of the three-inch-high spiked heel that was part of the costume worn by the cocktail waitresses at Rusty's Lounge. Rusty's Dive would have been a better name, Laura thought, not for the first time. The only lounging done in this place was when one of the patrons passed out and fell under a table. It was Friday night, and in another hour the place would be packed, but business was still slow enough that she had a few minutes to contemplate her life.

Which was really no more productive than contemplating her reflection. But it was her birthday, and it seemed as if she ought to spend a little time thinking about her life and where it was going. The answer was simple enough.

Nowhere. She was going absolutely nowhere.

The eyes in the mirror were bleak, older than they had any right to be. She was twenty-two today, and in heavy makeup she could have passed for thirty. There was nothing to look forward to but year after year of working in places like Rusty's, serving drinks and fending off passes, but not fending them off too vigorously because she counted on the tips to cover the gap that minimum wage left in her budget. Sooner or later, she'd stop fending them off at all.

Maybe she'd go home with a customer one night, telling herself that he might be the one to take her away from all this. He wouldn't be, so she'd tell herself that the next guy would be the one. Or the next, or the one after that. And when they smiled and tucked a few bills in her cleavage and told her to buy herself something pretty, she'd pretend that it was just a little present.

It's not like they're paying me for anything, Miss Pruneface. They're just bein' nice. They like me. If you were pretty, you might find out what I mean, but you won't never have to worry about men being nice to you 'cause of your looks.

Her mother's voice rang so vividly in her head that she nearly looked around to see if Billie Halloran was standing behind her. But her mother had been dead for three years now, run over by a car while she was lying in the middle of the street, too drunk to recognize the danger.

Laura's shiver had nothing to do with the temperature. She suddenly saw herself standing at the beginning of the path her mother had taken, a path she'd sworn would never be hers. Yet here she was, working in a bar, barely making ends meet and starting to feel as if her whole life were going to pass her by without her ever having really lived.

Was this how her mother had felt? Had she felt this same emptiness inside, a hollow certainty that life was probably never going to offer anything more than it already had? Laura closed her eyes, shutting out the bar, shutting out her own smoke-blurred reflection.

"Got a couple of customers by the back wall, Laura. They look like big tippers."

Laura opened her eyes and found the table Sally had indicated in the mirror. Two urban cowboys had settled at the round table, one turning the chair around so that he straddled it in a way he probably thought made him look macho.

"They look like jerks," Laura said. But she straightened away from the bar and slid her feet back into her shoes.

"Jerks sometimes leave the best tips—sort of God's way of apologizing to those of us who have to deal with them, I always think." Sally grinned and turned to give the bartender her order.

Laura made her way across the room, pinning on a friendly smile as she reached the table Sally had pointed out.

"What can I get you?"

"Well, now, just what are you offering?" The one who spoke was in his forties, his hair thinning and his belt fighting a losing battle with his belly. He was grinning at her as if he were sure he was the first one to ever try that line on a waitress and he just couldn't believe his own cleverness.

"We offer a full bar," she told him, taking the question at face value.

"What I got my eye on don't look like it'll fit in a glass," Mr. Clever said, leering openly at the cleavage framed by the ruffled neckline of her low-cut black dress.

"How about one of Rusty's Specials?" Laura offered, wondering if it would affect the amount of the tip if she brained him with her tray.

"If it's half as special as you, it must pack some wallop." He grinned at his companion, pleased with his unending stream of witticisms.

"Two Specials, then?" Laura felt as if her smile had been thumbtacked to her face.

"Yeah, sure. Just make sure *you* bring 'em, sugar. They wouldn't be special, otherwise." He was still chortling when Laura turned away, sidestepping in a quick, casual move that took her out of reach of patting hands and pinching fingers. Behind her, she heard a muttered curse, felt the brush of air against the short skirt of her costume and allowed herself a small, triumphant smile.

Her eyes collided with those of the man who'd seated himself in the booth at a right angle to Mr. Clever's table. She hadn't seen him before, so he'd obviously just sat down. It was equally obvious that he'd recognized her maneuver for what it was and was amused by it. Her steps faltered momentarily before she straightened her spine and stopped next to the booth.

"What can I get for you?"

"Four Roses, on the rocks." He reached up to run his fingers through his dark blond hair. Something in the movement spoke of bone-deep weariness.

"Sure thing." Laura turned away, not bothering to sidestep, knowing it wasn't necessary.

And it didn't become necessary as the evening wore on. Mr. Clever—*call me Randy, honey*—and his friend, whose only purpose in life seemed to be to encourage Randy's offensive behavior, stayed at their table, drinking steadily and growing steadily more obnoxious. The blond stranger ordered one drink for every three of theirs, cradling each between his hands, content to watch the ice melt.

As annoyed as Laura was with the two pretend cowboys, she found herself equally intrigued by the stranger with the pale eyes. She found herself wanting to know whether his eyes were blue or gray, wanting to know what he looked like when he smiled. Something about him suggested that he didn't smile a whole lot. She wasn't quite sure what it was that intrigued her. Maybe it was just the contrast between his behavior and that of the two men who sat a few feet from him. He didn't leer at her. His eyes never lingered on her breasts or dropped to the length of leg exposed by her short skirt. He thanked her when she brought his drinks and treated her like a human being. It was a marked contrast to good old Randy and company.

Laura allowed herself to speculate about him. It gave her something to think about besides the fact that it was her twenty-second birthday and there was no one who knew, no one who'd care if they did know. Maybe he was a talent scout from a major studio, looking for a not-particularly-pretty, not-at-all-talented unknown to play a major part in a major film.

No, he didn't look like the talent-scout type. She shook her head, frowning at her reflection over the bar as she waited for Dave to prepare her order. Something more outdoorsy, maybe. Not big enough for a football player, though there was certainly nothing shabby about the width of his shoulders. Construction work? Maybe. It wasn't hard to picture him perched on a catwalk in a half-finished building, shirtless, maybe, hammering a nail or something.

Maybe he was a private investigator. He'd come to Rusty's looking for her. That was it. Laura's eyes grew dreamy, focusing on her inner vision. She had a grandmother somewhere, a tall, elegant old woman who lived in a huge house, surrounded by devoted family retainers. Her grandmother had hired a P.I. to find her, a man who knew how to get information off "the street."

He'd been looking for her for months—maybe even years. No, make it months. After all, her grandmother would hire only the best. He was watching her, checking her resemblance to the old family portraits. Naturally, she was the image of her grandmother as a young woman.

Maybe he'd wait until her shift ended, just watching her with those pale eyes, and then he'd stop her as she was leaving and break the news that she had a family, someone who wanted her. In the fantasy, he was wearing a trench coat and his voice held a vaguely Bogartish edge. Or maybe it was a Hawaiian shirt and a pair of shorts. She frowned, hovering uncertainly between the two images.

"Hey. You gonna take these drinks before or after the ice melts?" Dave's impatient demand snapped her out of her daydream. Flushing, Laura took the drinks from the bartender and set them on her tray. Maybe she ought to concentrate on her job and forget about the man with the ice-colored eyes. He was probably an accountant, anyway.

* * *

Conner stared down into his drink and wished it were harder to remember what number this was. When he'd walked into Rusty's Lounge, it had been his firm intention to drink himself close enough to oblivion to guarantee that he'd sleep the rest of the night. He could have just bought a bottle and taken it back to his motel where he could have drunk himself into a stupor with straightforward efficiency. But for some reason he hadn't really wanted to be alone.

So he'd come here, only to find that his loneliness was something he carried inside, something that was a part of him even when he was in a crowded bar. And to top it off, he'd soon realized that he had little taste for the sort of heavy drinking that would provide him with the oblivion he craved.

Still, he'd lingered, though he wasn't sure why. There was nothing appealing about the place. Except maybe the waitress, he amended as she brought him another glass. She offered him a pleasant smile as she picked up his empty glass, emptied the ashtray and swiped a rag over the table before setting the fresh drink down in front of him.

Maybe he'd stayed because of her. She was wearing too much makeup, and the tacky little black costume she wore was so obviously intended to tantalize that it was ridiculous. But there was something in her eyes that stirred a response somewhere inside him. A loneliness, perhaps. A certain emptiness he thought he could relate to.

Conner's mouth twisted cynically. On the other hand, maybe there was nothing in her eyes but boredom and he was imagining everything he thought he'd

read there. She was probably happily married, had an
address book full of friends and didn't know the
meaning of lonely.

He wished he could say the same. If he'd thought
that getting away from the ranch would give him a
respite from the loneliness that rode on his shoulder
like an unwanted companion, he'd been wrong. His
memories came with him, especially here.

The last time he'd been in L.A., Rachel had been
with him. They'd taken a vacation the year after they
were married, and she'd wanted to come here and do
all the touristy things. Conner's taste ran more to mu-
seums and libraries, but he'd let her drag him to every
tourist trap the town had to offer—and Los Angeles
had plenty of them.

Remembering the sound of her laughter, he felt a
sudden, tight pain in his chest. Damn, but she'd loved
life. That was part of what made it impossible to let
go. It just didn't seem possible that all that laughter
was gone forever. He cursed under his breath and
lifted his glass to drain it, feeling the whiskey burn its
way to his belly.

Catching the waitress's eye, he signaled for another
drink. Her dark brows lifted in surprise at his request
coming so soon after she'd delivered the last one, but
she delivered a fresh drink promptly. Conner caught
her looking at him, a worried look in her blue eyes.
Worry for him or just concern that he was going to
become as obnoxious as the drunks at the next table?
he wondered as he watched her deftly evade a pat on
the butt as she set their drinks on the table.

He felt his upper lip curl as he watched the two men
and heard their crude remarks as she moved away.

They made no effort to lower their voices, and their comments were clearly audible over the blare of an old Conway Twitty song coming from the jukebox. From the way she was walking—like a poker had been thrust down her dress—Conner knew she'd heard the comments. He thought the color deepened in her cheeks, but it was difficult to be sure in the dim light.

Jerks. He had no patience with men who treated women the way these two were treating the waitress. When he was younger and hotter tempered, he'd probably have said something. But he was old enough and burned out enough not to care too much. No doubt, the woman was used to handling customers like them. She'd probably offer them a pleasant smile, dodge their groping hands and come away with a nice, fat tip that had cost her nothing more than a little annoyance. He focused his gaze on his drink and reminded himself to mind his own business.

But it wasn't annoyance he heard in her voice a moment later, it was anger and a touch of fear. "Let me go!"

Conner's head jerked up as a glass fell, shattering against the floor. She had apparently brought back their change for the bill they'd given her, and Randy's lust had finally gotten the better of him. He must have grabbed for her bodice. Whether he'd intended to tear it or she'd torn it when she jerked away was anybody's guess. But the end result was that the dress split from neckline to waist, exposing a soft white cotton bra that was not in keeping with the tacky little dress, and a wealth of silky, soft skin.

Too drunk or too stupid to be satisfied with the damage he'd already done, Randy grabbed for her as she spun away, catching her around the waist and dragging her back down into his lap, ignoring her struggles.

Conner was out of the booth in a heartbeat. Out the corner of his eye, he saw the bartender coming out from behind the bar, heading for the disturbance that had instantly riveted every eye in the place. Some distant, sober part of his mind suggested that he should sit back down, let the bartender handle the situation. It was his job to extricate the little waitress and deal with Randy and his pal, who was hooting his approval of his friend's actions.

But he was in no mood to listen to sober reason. Maybe it was the Four Roses. Maybe it was a need to escape the memories. Maybe it was just that he'd been longing to plow his fist into Randy's chunky features from the moment he'd sat down. Whatever it was, he didn't bother to wait for the bartender.

His hand closed over the waitress's slender wrist, hearing her startled cry as he jerked her up off the other man's lap and pulled her out of the way. The moment he released her, his left hand closed over the front of Randy's shirt. He yanked the other man to his feet, letting his own momentum carry Randy's face into his fist.

Chapter 2

It all happened so fast that afterward, Laura wasn't sure just what *did* happen. One minute, she was struggling furiously with Randy. The next, she'd been pulled away from him with enough force that momentum carried her several feet away from the table.

Holding her torn bodice to her chest, she reached up to push the hair back from her eyes. Before the gesture was completed, she heard the solid thunk of a fist connecting with someone's jaw. She shoved her hair out of her face in time to see Randy collapse to the floor like a felled ox. Standing over him, his hands still clenched, was the stranger with the pale eyes.

And that should have been the end of the incident. It would have been the end of it if Randy's companion hadn't taken exception to his friend's defeat.

"You can't do that, you bastard."

"I just did." There was a feral gleam in the stranger's eyes, something in his stance that challenged. It was a challenge the other man was just drunk enough to accept.

"Hold it!" Dave's harried voice preceded him as he attempted to push his way through the crowd that had gathered. He was too late to stop Randy's buddy from launching himself at Randy's opponent. He was bigger than his friend and considerably bigger than the stranger, outweighing him by at least thirty pounds, and most of it was muscle.

Laura caught her breath as he lunged forward, afraid that she was going to see her unexpected defender flattened. But instead of meeting the attack head-on, he waited until the other man was almost on him and then sidestepped quickly. The simple move was both unexpected and effective. His opponent plunged past him and into the crowd, aided by the judicious application of a booted foot to his rear end.

There was scattered laughter, and Laura drew a cautious breath, thinking that the incident was finished.

Afterward, she wasn't sure what had happened. Maybe someone took exception to having their toes stepped on. Or maybe Randy's friend, having failed in his initial objective, chose a new target. It was impossible to see who threw the first punch, who shoved who. But in the space between one breath and the next, a full-blown brawl was breaking out.

Conner ducked under a punch, blocked a second with his forearm and swung a right to his opponent's jaw. He had no idea who he was fighting or why. And he didn't care. The feel of his fist connecting with good ole' Randy's chin had done more to improve Conner's mood than a full bottle of whiskey could have. He wasn't averse to continuing the fight as long as there was someone interested in bringing it to him.

He felt someone grab his arm and jerked away from the hold, fists raised as he turned to face the new threat. But it wasn't a burly construction worker who'd grabbed him. It was the little waitress, her eyes wide and frightened. She reached for his arm again. She was saying something, but it was impossible to hear anything over the noise in the bar.

Conner resisted as she pulled him toward a hallway near the back of the bar. He guessed it led to a door, but he wasn't particularly interested in leaving. It might be stupid, but he was enjoying the fight and in no mood to abandon it. He started to pull away from her, but like a limpet she clung with one hand, cupping her other hand to her ear and then pointing to the front door.

Frowning, Conner tried to pick out a sound above the shouts and curses and the crisp ring of shattered glass. It took him a moment to hear what she was trying to tell him. Sirens. Someone had called the police. And she was trying to get him out of here before he ended up spending the night in jail, not to mention the possibility of a hefty fine.

Seeing the comprehension in his eyes, she released her hold on his arm and started toward the back door, skirting the fight that still raged in the center of the room. Conner detoured long enough to grab his jacket from the booth, slinging the sheepskin-lined denim over his shoulder.

They'd almost reached the hallway when someone grabbed Conner's shoulder, spinning him around. And there was Randy, his pudgy face red and twisted with anger, his jaw swollen and a cut over one eyebrow that was bleeding freely. He was saying something, the words lost in the roar of the fight, but Conner didn't have to hear what he was saying to know that Randy was calling his ancestry into question, not to mention his sexual proclivities and probably his bathing habits.

Randy seemed the type who had to talk before he could act. If he'd simply started out swinging, he could have landed at least one good punch before Conner had a chance to get his hands up. Instead, he stood there, yammering on, enamored of the sound of his own voice, even when he couldn't hear it.

He was still talking when Conner's fist caught him under the chin. The click of his teeth slamming together could be felt even though it couldn't be heard. The force of the punch lifted him onto his toes. His eyes glazed over before rolling back in his head. And for the second time that evening, he dropped to the floor like a sack of grain.

Conner had only a moment to savor the image before he felt the little waitress tug on his arm again. Since the scream of sirens was clearly audible now, he didn't hesitate but turned and followed her down the dingy hallway and out the back door. The door shut behind them, cutting off the sound of the fight. But the sirens were painfully loud.

"Come on. They'll block the alley." Her voice was breathless, and her fingers dug into his sleeve as if she were willing to try physically dragging him.

Though he felt no particular urgency—courtesy, no doubt, of the Four Roses—Conner allowed her to pull him down the alley and onto a side street. She really shouldn't be running in those high heels, he thought, watching her ankles wobble as the spiky heels threatened to twist out from under her. She was likely to end up with a sprained ankle. Still, he couldn't deny that the ridiculous shoes did something for her legs—nice, long legs for such a little thing.

They were only a few yards away from the alley when a police car turned the corner in front of them, siren screaming and red lights flashing. He felt his companion tense and slid his arm around her shoulders, slowing her quick steps to a more casual pace.

"We're just out for a stroll," he said. "No reason for the police to be interested in us."

An instant later, the black-and-white went by them and turned into the alley. The tension left her so abruptly that, for a moment, she actually leaned against him, as if not sure her knees would support her. She was a soft, feminine weight, stirring feelings he'd suppressed for a long time. But she allowed herself only a moment's weakness.

"I think we're safe enough now," she said, still sounding breathless. She straightened up and away from him, and Conner was aware of a vague disappointment.

They continued walking until they turned the corner. She stopped in front of a pawnshop, closed for the night, its windows covered with a steel grill. Conner had no idea what time it was, but he knew it must be late.

They stood together without speaking, looking at each other, uncertain of what to say or do next. Conner was feeling better than he had in months—years maybe. The adrenaline generated by the fight had dissipated, leaving behind a kind of nervous energy, a feeling of being intensely alive.

She shivered, and it occurred to him that the skimpy costume she wore offered little by way of warmth. Compared to what he was used to, the temperature was almost balmy. But it was a mite chilly to be standing around in a garment that covered little more than a bathing suit.

She was still holding the torn bodice up with one hand, and he had a sudden memory of a glimpse of pale skin and an innocent white cotton bra that was so at odds with the tacky black dress. He pushed the memory away and slid his jacket off his shoulders.

"Here." He slung the denim jacket around her. She stiffened for a moment, and he thought she might refuse. But then she snuggled into its warmth, tugging it closed across her breasts. "Thank you." She gave him a shy smile, and he had the feeling that it had been a long time since anyone had offered her much by way of simple courtesies.

"You're welcome. I'm Conner Fox." He held out his hand.

"Laura Halloran." Her hand was small, the fingers delicate and fragile in his. She stirred feelings he'd almost forgotten, an urge to protect, a need to shelter her, keep her safe. Not to mention a touch of basic lust. Had to be the whiskey, he thought.

"I want to thank you for coming to my rescue in there," she said.

"My pleasure."

His smile held a wicked edge that Laura felt all the way to her toes. She'd wondered what he'd look like when he smiled, and now she knew. There ought to be an ordinance against smiles with that kind of impact. She swallowed and tried to look as if she weren't suddenly breathless.

"Well, I guess I should go home. I don't think the police are going to let them open up again tonight."

"I'd guess not. I'll walk you home."

"That's not necessary."

"Sure it is. You shouldn't be walking around by yourself at this hour of the night. Besides, my truck was parked in front of the bar and I don't think it's a real good idea to lay claim to it right now. Too many people might be willing to point me out as the one who started the fight."

"You didn't start the fight," she protested. "It was that pig, Randy, who started it."

"Well that's how you see it, and I have to admit to taking that point of view myself." He grinned at her again, and Laura felt her knees weaken. "But I suspect there are those who might be uncharitable enough to mention that I threw the first punch."

"He deserved it," she muttered.

"I agree with you there, too. But I still think it wouldn't be in my best interest to introduce myself to the police at this point."

"No, of course not. My apartment is just a few blocks away. I usually catch a ride home with Sally. She's one of the other waitresses. I wasn't really looking forward to walking home alone," she admitted, giving him that shy smile again.

Conner fell into step beside her, slowing his pace to match her shorter strides. He felt better than he had any business feeling. Somewhere in the back of his mind, he considered the probability that he wouldn't feel good at all come morning. He was past the age where he could drink all night, get into a brawl and not feel it in the morning. But he wasn't going to worry about that now. He was simply going to enjoy the cool night air and the soft, feminine company of the woman beside him.

Laura was tempted to go past her apartment building when they reached it. The walk seemed much too short. She'd enjoyed having Conner Fox beside her, enjoyed the sheer masculine presence of him. It seemed a shame that it had to end. But she could hardly lead him around the block half a dozen times.

"Well, this is it." She stopped in front of the unprepossessing stucco building and turned to look at him. "It was very nice of you to walk me home."

"It was no trouble." Conner looked down at her, aware that he was reluctant to let her go. It had been a long time since he'd felt any real desire for company other than his own. "Any idea how long before it'll be safe for me to go back and get my truck?"

He didn't expect her to know the answer any more than he did, but it was a way to delay saying good night, to postpone the moment when he'd have to walk away. To put off the loneliness that had been his only real companion for so long now.

"An hour or so, at least. They'll take statements and decide whether or not they're going to arrest anyone. It takes them awhile."

''You sound like you've been through this before. Are fights a regular part of the entertainment?''

''Not really. This is only the second one in the year I've been there.''

''Sounds downright tame.''

They lingered, Laura standing on the step, Conner on the sidewalk. The position put her almost eye to eye with him, and she found herself wondering again just what color his eyes were. The fitful light from a nearby street lamp was not strong enough to reveal their color. If he walked away now, she'd never know.

''I could make you a cup of coffee.'' The words startled her, and she pressed her fingers against her mouth as if she could somehow call them back.

''Coffee sounds nice.'' Those pale eyes raked over her face, reading the uncertainty in her expression. ''If you're sure you want to invite me in.''

''I...'' She started to say that she wasn't at all sure, but she felt the weight of his jacket around her shoulders and remembered his quiet courtesy when she'd brought him his drinks. ''I'm sure.''

Conner followed her up two flights of stairs, telling himself that it was purely academic interest that kept his eyes focused on the gentle sway of her hips. There was a run in her black stockings, and he followed the path of it from her ankle, along the soft curve of her calf, past her knee and up the back of her thigh until it disappeared beneath the ruffled hem of her dress. It was a considerable length of leg for such a small woman, more than enough to wrap around a man's waist.

''I keep a key under the flowerpot because I sometimes forget mine.'' Laura's voice made him drag his eyes away from the enticing length of her legs. It had to be the whiskey. He couldn't remember the last time he'd felt any real interest in a woman, no matter how great her legs were.

She slid her fingers under the base of a plastic potted plant that sat in the hallway outside her apartment door. It had a dusty look that matched its surroundings. The building had definitely seen better days, though it had never been a showplace.

Laura was acutely aware of Conner as she pushed open the apartment door and stepped through. The door opened directly into the living room, which became the bedroom when the sofa was pulled out into a bed. There was a small kitchen and an even smaller bathroom, all of it painted a dull shade that looked as if it hadn't quite decided to be beige but was unwilling to commit to being white.

Laura had added throw pillows in bright colors and potted plants crowded the sill of the single window. There was a brightly colored floral print on one wall in a cheap enameled frame and a throw rug in vivid shades of blue and purple on the floor in front of the sofa. It made the room look a little less like it was part of a barracks, but nothing could disguise the shabbiness of the apartment.

"If you'd like to have a seat, it'll just take me a second to put on something that isn't torn." She gave him a quick, uncertain smile and disappeared into the bathroom.

Conner stared at the door for a moment, finding it remarkably easy to picture her undressing behind it. Would she leave on that prim little bra or would she take it off? With her coloring, he'd be willing to bet that her nipples were a dusky rose color that would stand out against the pale mound of her breast.

"Damn!" He spun on one heel, putting his back to the door as if that would be enough to stop the pictures his imagination seemed only too eager to paint. He tugged at the fly of his jeans, trying to ease the uncomfortable pressure of his arousal. If he had any sense—any sense at all—he'd walk out right now before that door opened again, before he had a chance to see those big blue eyes and those long, long legs again.

But he didn't move toward the door. Something stronger than common sense kept him where he was. He didn't want to be alone again. Not tonight. He'd spent so many nights alone. Surely he was entitled to just one night without ghosts and memories. Just someone to talk to, someone to share the dark hours before dawn—that wasn't too much to ask, was it?

Laura's fingers were shaking as she stripped off her ruined dress. She'd probably have to pay for it, she thought, kicking it aside. The fact that a customer had torn it wasn't going to move Rusty to take responsibility for its destruction. But at the moment, she didn't care about the dress or the fact that its cost would come out of her paycheck. Right now, all she could think about was the man waiting for her on the other side of the scuffed door.

Conner Fox. The name had a solid sound to it. Like the man it belonged to. Solid and all male. Most definitely all male. The kind of man who made a woman's heart beat a little fast, the kind of man who tended to figure in a woman's fantasies.

She reached for the jeans and T-shirt she'd pulled out of the closet on the way into the bathroom and tugged them on. But then she hesitated. She stared at the bathroom door and nibbled her lower lip. A few short hours ago, she'd been thinking about what a rut she'd fallen into; of how life was passing her by.

Her eyes lifted to meet those of her reflection in the mirror over the sink. She'd certainly been bounced right out of that rut tonight. A man had fought for her, had defended her honor—to use an old-fashioned phrase. And not just any man, but a man to fulfill more than a few dreams.

He was in her living room, just a few feet away, waiting for her. She'd make a cup of coffee, they'd share a few minutes of polite conversation and then he'd leave and she'd never see him again. The thought brought a wave of panic all out of proportion to what she had any right to feel. She barely knew the man.

So why did she feel as if she were on a sinking ship and he was manning the last lifeboat?

"I have some brandy, if you'd prefer," Laura said as she left the bathroom.

"Brandy sounds fine." He dropped the magazine he'd picked up back onto the stack he'd taken it from and watched her cross to the alcove that contained the kitchen.

Laura was acutely aware of his eyes on her as she opened the cupboard to find the bottle of brandy. It was on the third shelf up and she rose on her toes, stretching her hand to reach it.

"Let me get it." Conner's voice came from just behind her, and she felt his body brush against hers as he reached over her head, lifting the slim bottle from the shelf.

"Thank you." She took it from him, clutching it against her chest as she turned. He'd stepped back, but he was still close—so close that she could feel the heat of his body, close enough for her to see that his eyes weren't gray or blue. They were green, a clear, icy shade of green that seemed to see right into her, making her feel naked and vulnerable and tremblingly aware of the basic differences between male and female.

"It's not very expensive brandy," she said to fill the silence. "I bought it after I read a recipe in a magazine for a flaming dessert. It looked so pretty in the photograph that I wanted to try it."

"How did it turn out?"

"Awful." Her smile made her nose wrinkle. "I nearly set fire to my hair and then I couldn't get the flames to die down. I think I put too much brandy in. So I threw a glass of water on it because I was afraid it would set off the smoke detector. Anyway, I didn't feel like trying it again, so I ended up with this bottle of brandy left and nothing to do with it.

"I don't have snifters," she said as she handed him a juice glass full of amber liquid. "I hope this will do."

"It's fine."

Conner followed her to the sofa, sitting down beside her. She'd been chattering a moment ago, but she seemed to have abruptly run out of things to say. The silence was not uncomfortable, at least not to him. He was feeling very relaxed and loose—the result of both the whiskey and the fight and maybe the proximity of the woman beside him.

"Do you live near here?" she asked after a moment.

"About a thousand miles east of here," he said, leaning his head back on the sofa and giving in to the lazy contentment. "I have a ranch in Colorado."

She could almost have guessed as much. Everything about him said that this was no urban cowboy, but the real thing. She sipped her brandy, feeling the heavy liquid burn its way down her throat before settling in a warm pool in the pit of her stomach.

"Do you raise cows?"

Conner's grin was a quick slash of white against his tanned skin. It did more to raise her temperature than any amount of brandy could have.

"Cattle," he said. "Dairy farmers raise cows. Ranchers raise cattle."

"What's the difference?"

"It's more a matter of image than anything else. You just can't picture John Wayne moving a thousand head of cows up from Texas." He shook his head, that grin tugging at the corners of his mouth and sending a tingle up Laura's spine. She took another quick swallow of brandy to banish the urge to reach out and put her fingers against his mouth, to feel his smile as well as see it.

"Okay, do you raise cattle on your ranch?" she asked equably.

"A few. My main business is raising and training quarter horses."

"Quarter horses? Why would anyone want a quarter of a horse?" The laughter in her eyes gave the lie to her solemn mouth.

"I get the feeling that you haven't spent a lot of time in the country."

"Not unless you count a trip to the L.A. County Fair when I was eleven." She paused and sipped her brandy before giving him an impish look. "But I only saw whole horses there, no halves or quarters."

Conner's chuckle was rusty sounding, as if he didn't use it very often. Laura felt it sink inside her, adding to the warmth of the brandy. She lifted her glass to her mouth. The brandy no longer burned her throat. Instead, it seemed to flow down like sun-warmed honey, pooling inside her, heating her body from fingertips to toes.

Conner's smile faded, his dark brows coming together in a frown. He reached out, catching her hand and drawing it toward him. Following his gaze, Laura saw the faint blue marks that marked her wrist. His frown deepened as he fit his fingers over the marks, his thumb overlapping his forefinger by a more than comfortable margin.

"Did I do that when I pulled you away from what's his name?"

"I bruise easily," she said, by way of answer. She could have pulled her hand back, but she let it stay where it was, enjoying the feeling of him touching her, even if it was in a relatively impersonal way.

But there was nothing impersonal about the feel of his lips on the inside of her wrist. She sucked in a quick breath, her eyes going wide as she stared at his bent head. He was just being kind, she told herself. He couldn't know that the simple gesture sent shock waves through her.

He lifted his head, those clear green eyes catching
hers. His fingers shifted subtly, and she knew he could
feel the way her pulse skittered under the light touch.
She swallowed, feeling her mouth go dry. In a heartbeat, the atmosphere had changed. Or maybe this
tension—this awareness—had been there all along and
they'd just been pretending it wasn't.

"Your skin is so pale." His thumb brushed over the
soft flesh of her inner wrist in a slow rhythm.

"I don't get out in the sun much, I guess. Working
nights, you know, and then sleeping late. Besides, too
much sun isn't good for you." She hardly knew what
she was saying. Conner didn't say anything when she
stopped, only continued to watch her with those pale
green eyes and stroke her skin with that maddeningly
light touch.

"It's my birthday." She blurted the information
out, needing to break the silence. "I mean, it *was* my
birthday. Since it's after midnight now...." The words
trailed off in a little gasp as his hand slid up her arm,
pulling her forward, closing the gap between them.

"Happy birthday."

"Th-thank you." She swallowed hard, feeling her
heart beating in her throat. Her tongue came out to
wet her lower lip and she saw his eyes drop to the
movement.

"Did you get a birthday kiss?" he asked huskily.

"N-no." She swallowed again, her throat moving
convulsively. He was going to kiss her. Or he would if
she let him. She couldn't be thinking about letting
him, could she?

''Everyone should get a birthday kiss,'' he whispered, so close she could feel his breath against her skin.

She was going to pull away. Any second now, she'd draw back, maybe with a sophisticated little laugh to show that she didn't take any of this seriously. She wouldn't—couldn't—just sit here and let him kiss her.

And then his lips brushed against hers in a featherlight kiss, so soft she could almost have believed that she imagined it. He drew back, his eyes searching hers, asking questions she wasn't quite sure of, getting answers she didn't know she was giving.

There was no doubting the reality of the next kiss. His mouth settled over hers as if claiming it for his own. And she surrendered to that claim without a protest. It was as if this were the moment she'd spent her life waiting for. Her mouth opened to him as her hands came up to grasp his arms, clinging to him as the world swayed around her.

His tongue traced the fullness of her lower lip, teased at the barrier of her teeth and then slid inside. He withdrew, only to thrust forward again, claiming her mouth in an age-old rhythm. Laura shuddered, her fingers digging into the hard muscles of his arms. Her tongue came up to twine with his as she melted closer to him, craving a deeper contact.

When Conner broke the kiss, they were both breathless. He stared at her, his eyes ice-green and hot as a furnace as they raked over her flushed features. Laura stared at him, dazed by what was happening. It was only a kiss, she reminded herself. Just a kiss. But her heart was pounding and she felt an ache in the pit of her stomach, a hunger she'd never known before.

"I want you."

The stark words slammed into her, stealing her breath away, adding to the ache lodged inside her.

"I—" She didn't know what she'd planned to say. Her thoughts were spinning too fast. But his mouth swallowed the words, his tongue stabbing deep into her mouth. Laura's breath left her on a soft whimper and she lifted one hand to his head, her fingers sliding into the thick, dark gold of his hair, pulling him closer, wanting to lose herself in the kiss.

When he lifted his head again, she was sprawled across his lap with no memory of how she'd come to be there. His hand was beneath her T-shirt, flattened on the bare skin of her midriff. Laura stared up at him, dazed by the quick rise of passion, by the depth of her own hunger.

"I want you," he said again. Something in his eyes told her that he was as surprised as she was by what was happening. There was something reassuring about that surprise.

She opened her mouth, but all that came out was a shocked little exhalation as his hand shifted, closing over her breast. She'd taken off her bra since the T-shirt provided perfectly adequate coverage. But she hadn't anticipated having Conner Fox put his hand under her shirt; couldn't have anticipated the wave of sensation that shot through her at the feel of his hand covering her breast. His thumb brushed her nipple, and Laura was helpless to stop the soft moan that rose in her throat.

"You're so soft. So incredibly soft." The words were a whisper against her throat as his hand worked its magic. And then he was pushing the T-shirt up, baring her to his gaze. Laura might have protested then, more in embarrassment than anything else, but he bent his head and stroked his tongue across one swollen peak and she was lost.

In that moment, she gave up any thought of stopping what was happening. Later, she'd tell herself it was the brandy or the confused feelings generated by her birthday. But in the here and now, all she knew was that nothing in her life had ever felt so completely right.

For one blindingly clear moment, she knew exactly what she was about to do. She looked at it with clear eyes and made her choice. There'd almost certainly be regrets later, maybe big ones, but this was a chance she had to take. She couldn't have said why, but for once in her life she was going to let her instincts dictate her path and the devil take the future.

Her skin was even softer than he'd imagined. Her breasts were milky white with dusky pink crests that pebbled beneath the stroke of his tongue. Conner tasted her response in the way she trembled against him, felt it in the way her thighs unconsciously clenched and unclenched, seeking to soothe the deep feminine ache he'd started.

He drew her nipple into his mouth, sucking strongly. At the same time, his hand slid down the soft curve of her belly to cup the heart of her. His touch scorched her even through the fabric of her jeans. She arched into his hand, her legs opening to him in invitation.

Somewhere inside him, a tiny voice suggested that things were moving too fast, that he should stop and think about what he was doing. But Conner let the gut-deep hunger smother it. He didn't want to think about the past or future.

His fingers were impatient with the zipper on her jeans, but it finally yielded and his hand slid inside the denim, inside the thin nylon of her panties to cup her core. She was all heat and dampness, as hungry for this as he was.

It was too quick, he thought. He should take more time. But his hands were already stripping her jeans away. Somehow, she was lying beneath him on the old sofa, and his fingers were shaking as he strove to work loose the buttons on his jeans. His shirt had disappeared—he couldn't remember when and didn't care. All that mattered was that, for a little while at least, he wasn't alone. There was someone to share the night, someone to hold the memories at bay.

He stripped his jeans down his long legs, barely hearing Laura's soft gasp when she saw the hard strength of his arousal. He settled back against her, nudging at the damp warmth of her. Wrapping his hands in her hair, he tilted her head back, his eyes burning into hers. Seeing the uncertainty in hers, he forced himself to stillness, though every nerve in his body was screaming for him to complete the union that lay so close.

"If this isn't what you want, say it now." Strain made the words guttural, but he meant them. It would damn near kill him to do it, but it would only take one word to end it here and now.

"No." The word could have meant anything. No, this wasn't what she wanted. Or no, she didn't want him to stop. But there was no mistaking the gentle undulation of her hips, the silent plea in the way her fingers clung to his upper arms.

"Yes." The word hissed between his teeth as he allowed himself to settle against her.

Hot silk surrounded him, a pleasure so intense, it was nearly pain. She enfolded him tight as a glove, all damp heat and softness. Groaning, he lowered his mouth to hers and completed the embrace with a slow, deep thrust.

The thin barrier was breached even as he registered its existence. She cried out, the sound disappearing in his kiss. Her nails bit into his arms as she arched against him, deepening the embrace, whether intentionally or not, he couldn't judge.

Buried in the supple sheath of her body, he didn't move. His thoughts were disjointed. A virgin. The possibility hadn't even crossed his mind. No wonder she was so tight around him. He was the first man to share her body. There was something primitive in him that responded to that knowledge, some deep, male need to claim a woman as his and his alone.

But this wasn't part of the bargain, wasn't what he'd anticipated. This wasn't a few moments of forgetfulness, an easing of the loneliness he'd sensed she shared. This was more than he'd asked, more than he could accept. He tensed and drew back, intending to end it here and now.

She tightened around him, her body sheathing his as if made for him alone. The sweet pressure was irresistible. With a groan, he thrust home, feeling her surround him, welcome him. The sensation was more than he could fight. It had been so long, such a damned, aching long time. And she felt so good. So completely right.

Laura had been sure she knew what she was doing. She'd made a calm, rational decision that this night—this man—was the right night, the right man. She might not have experienced sex personally, but she knew all about it—no one who read a book or went to a movie in this day and age could possibly think sex was a mystery.

But nothing could have prepared her for the incredible intimacy of sharing her body with a man. There was the physical sensation, the feeling of being stretched, filled in ways she'd never known, but beyond that was the deep, visceral knowledge that everything had changed—she was changed.

He moved within her and she bit her lip against the lingering twinge of discomfort, but there was something more, something that made the discomfort a distant thing. There was a feeling that something incredible lay just beyond her reach, that she strained toward something bright and shining.

Conner suddenly stiffened above her, driving deep and hard, the tendons in his neck standing out as he threw his head back. Laura felt him swell and throb inside her and slid her arms around him as he shuddered in completion. Whatever she'd sought was destined to remain out of reach, but she felt oddly fulfilled by his pleasure, as if she'd given him a gift and gained something in the giving.

He collapsed against her, his breathing deep and ragged, his skin sheened with sweat. Laura held him, stroking her hands slowly up his back. She felt no regrets, no uncertainties. This was right, and for the moment, at least, she wasn't going to question how or why.

She was just going to accept the reality of it.

Chapter 3

Conner felt reality creep in around the edges of the most intense physical contentment he'd ever known. He tried to push it away, tried to ignore it. All he wanted was to lay his head on the sofa cushion beside Laura's and go to sleep. He wanted to spend what was left of the night right here, with his arms full of a living, breathing woman instead of trying to hold a memory.

But no matter how he tried to avoid it, those memories were intruding.

Rachel. My God, how could he have forgotten her?

He eased his weight from Laura, ashamed at his body's reluctance to leave hers, ashamed to acknowledge that if he let it happen, he could have made love to her again. What the hell was he thinking? Or was it that he hadn't thought at all?

He sat up on the edge of the sofa. Bracing his elbows on his knees, then dropped his head into his hands, feeling the beginnings of a pounding headache behind his eyes. It was the first time he'd ever gotten a hangover without waiting for the morning after. Or was it guilt that was making his head ache and his stomach roll?

As the silence stretched, he felt Laura move, drawing her legs up under her as she scrunched herself into the corner of the sofa as far away from him as it was possible to get. She tugged the bright crocheted afghan that lay across the back of the sofa and drew it across her body.

Conner saw the movement out the corner of his eye and his first thought was that her skin was too soft for the scratchy wool. The thought of just how soft her skin was brought a predictable response. He'd barely left her and he already wanted her again. The thought made him shoot to his feet and grab his jeans off the floor. He jammed his long legs into them, tugging them up around his hips and buttoning them with quick, jerky movements.

With that done, he let his hands drop to his sides. He wanted to walk out the door and pretend this night had never happened. He wanted to go back to the moment an hour ago when she'd invited him in for coffee and this time he'd refuse the offer. Or the moment when he'd first kissed her. Or... But there was no going back. What was done was done.

And, God help him, he wanted nothing so much as to do it again.

* * *

Laura watched the taut line of Conner's back as he sat on the edge of the sofa, and she wondered what he was thinking. It had been so wonderful. She'd felt completed, made whole in a way she'd never known was possible. It was crazy. She barely knew this man and yet she felt as if she'd known him forever, as if she'd been waiting for him.

But as the seconds ticked by and he didn't say anything, she felt the fragile contentment start to waver around the edges. She sat up and reached for the afghan she'd crocheted last winter and draped over the sofa to try and brighten the worn upholstery. The cheap yarn was rough against her skin, but she hardly noticed the discomfort. She was suddenly feeling very naked, very vulnerable.

Laura flinched when he shot to his feet and grabbed his jeans. There was suppressed violence in his movements as he pulled the jeans over his lean hips and buttoned them. She'd never watched a man dress before, and it struck her suddenly as almost unbearably intimate. She turned her head away and drew the afghan closer around her shoulders.

The silence stretched, and she slid her eyes back to him. He was simply standing there, his hands hanging at his sides, his shoulders slumped as if in defeat. There was an indefinable aloneness in his posture—as if he'd been alone forever and would never be anything but alone.

Laura shivered, feeling as if she'd been shut completely from his mind. She was suddenly uncertain about what she'd done. It had seemed so right, as if there were no real choice to make. Now it didn't seem clear at all.

My God, was this how her mother had felt the first time she'd gone home with a man she met in the bar? Had she told herself that it felt right, put some metaphysical twist on it to justify filling a lonely hour or two with another warm body?

Laura suddenly felt physically sick.

"Look, I—" Conner turned toward her.

"I'd like you to go, please."

She cut across his words, not wanting to hear him say he was sorry or tell her he really liked her but he had to be going now and he'd call her in the morning. How many times had she lain in bed and listened to some man give her mother the same farewell speech? And then the door would close behind him and there'd be the clink of a bottle against glass and she'd know that Billie was trying to wash away the taste of what she'd become.

"Laura, we need to talk."

"I'd like you to go. Now." She didn't want to talk. There was nothing to say.

"But I—"

"Please." She whispered the word, huddling deeper under the afghan, focusing her gaze somewhere beyond him. Her stomach was rolling and she could feel cold sweat breaking out on her forehead.

Conner stared at her, feeling frustration and relief in equal measure. They had to talk about what had just happened, but she'd made it clear that she wanted him gone, and he was ashamed to admit to a cowardly feeling of relief that the talk could be put off.

He stomped his feet into his boots and shrugged his shirt on but didn't bother to button it. Lifting his denim jacket from the chair where she'd put it, he hesitated, looking at her. She looked so small and vulnerable, so alone.

"Laura." He waited until she'd lifted her eyes to his and nearly winced at the bruised look in them. He wanted to go to her and take her in his arms. But he couldn't do that. "I'll be back."

"Fine." It was impossible to tell whether she believed him.

Cursing under his breath, Conner let himself out, wishing there was someone to blame for what had happened. But the guilt lay squarely on his shoulders. He was going to have to learn to live with it.

Laura watched the door close gently behind him. She felt almost completely numb. *I'll be back.* He wouldn't be, of course. Any number of her mother's lovers had promised to return, and they never did. Oh, some of them had come back a few times but then, why shouldn't they? Billie Halloran had been a pretty woman and for the right price she was usually willing. When she was young, the price had been a smile and a promise of affection. As the years wore on, she'd begun to think in terms of cash or some trinket that could be pawned to buy a bottle of whiskey.

She'd taken the first step, Laura thought. She pulled the afghan closer around her, almost grateful for the scratchy discomfort of it. Conner Fox hadn't even had to say he loved her. He'd only had to say that he wanted her. And she'd been so pathetically lonely that she'd accepted that as reason enough to take him as a lover—her first lover.

Tears stung her eyes, burning through the cold numbness she felt. She rolled her head to the side, pressing her face against the back of the sofa. The upholstery held a musty smell that she'd never been able to completely banish, but for once, she didn't even notice it.

She'd been a fool to think that sleeping with Conner Fox would make her feel less alone. If she were lucky, she'd never see him again, never be reminded of her own weakness. Which didn't explain the fact that she'd have given almost anything to have him walk back in the door and take her in his arms. But that would never happen. No doubt, she'd get her first wish and never see him again.

If Conner could have silenced his nagging conscience, Laura's guess might have been right. He'd have given a great deal to be able to sweep the entire night under a mental rug and pretend it had never happened. He'd never had much interest in casual sex, even before his marriage. Since Rachel's death, there'd been no one.

For a long time, grief had left no room for anything else. And when the first intensity of it had eased, he'd found he no longer had the taste for seeking out some woman with whom to spend a few pleasant hours now and again. Because that's all it could ever be. He was certainly never going to love another woman. The risk was too great, the cost too high.

He'd sublimated his sexual urges by putting in long hours doing hard, physical labor. And if he sometimes felt restless—ready to howl, as Gun would have put it—he just worked until physical exhaustion overrode the normal, healthy needs of a man his age.

Instead of going to Rusty's, he should have gone for a swim in the motel swimming pool. But he hadn't and what was done was done. There was no going back and no pretending it hadn't happened.

He drummed his fingers on the steering wheel of his truck and stared at the building across the street. If it had looked shabby in the dark, it looked downright ratty with the bright afternoon sun spilling over it, revealing the peeling paint and chipped stucco with merciless clarity. He'd had no trouble finding the place. He'd been drunk a week ago, but his sense of direction had been working just fine. Too bad his common sense hadn't been functioning, as well, he thought sourly.

Conner shoved the truck's door open and stepped down into the street. Slamming it behind him, he started across the cracked pavement, his long, lazy stride revealing none of the tension that roiled in his gut. It might be cowardly, but he'd have preferred to have this meeting on more neutral territory. The room that comprised Laura's apartment, the room where he'd made love to her, was hardly his idea of the ideal location for discussing what had happened between them.

But when he'd gone to Rusty's, hoping to catch her just as her shift was starting, he'd been informed that she no longer worked there. She'd been fired, the bartender had told him. She'd quit, was the opinion of a waitress with brassy red hair and a wad of gum the size of Pike's Peak. She'd glared at the bartender when she said it, and the look he gave her suggested that their enmity went back a long way. Conner had thanked them for the information and left. He was only interested in knowing that Laura no longer worked at Rusty's Lounge. The reasons could wait until later.

Which was how he'd ended up climbing the two flights of stairs to an apartment he'd have given a great deal to be able to forget. When he reached the second floor, he turned right and stopped in front of her door. Once there, he glared at the dusty plastic plant and tried to imagine what he was going to say to her.

Remember me? I'm the man you slept with a few nights ago.

Hi. Just thought I'd drop by and mention that I don't have any social diseases, and by the way, you couldn't possibly be pregnant, could you?

The latter thought brought a film of dampness to his forehead. God, how could he have been such a totally irresponsible fool? What was he going to do if he'd made her pregnant? It had taken Rachel almost three years to get pregnant. Surely fate couldn't be so unkind as for it take only once with a total stranger—a virginal stranger at that.

Wincing at the memory, Conner lifted his hand and knocked briskly on the door. Any hope he'd had that she wouldn't be home was dashed when he heard movement on the other side of the door and then her voice, low and husky, as if she might have been asleep.

"Who is it?"

"Conner Fox." He added nothing to the flat identification, knowing it would have been superfluous. He had no doubt that the events of last week were as indelibly branded in her mind as they were in his.

There was a moment of silence, and he didn't need X-ray vision to see the indecision on her face as she debated whether or not to open the door. He said nothing, having no doubts about the outcome of her mental argument. The scrape of the dead bolt being turned back sounded reluctant. The door swung open, and he stood face-to-face with Laura.

She stared at him, her teeth chewing her lower lip. He met her gaze, trying not to show the shock he felt at her changed appearance. The woman he'd met in the bar, the woman he'd made love to, had been in her late twenties. She'd looked like someone who'd been around the block a few times, which had made it an even greater shock to find that she hadn't even made it out the door, let alone around the block.

The woman staring at him seemed hardly deserving of the title. Girl was more like it. She wore no makeup, and her face had the fresh, scrubbed look of a schoolgirl. Her skin was pale, with a translucence that no amount of money could purchase once it had faded. Without the thick layer of eye shadow and mascara, her eyes looked larger, softer, reflecting a vulnerability that made him feel like a scoundrel.

"Can I come in?"

"Sure." She stepped back from the door, shutting it behind him and flipping the lock shut as he entered the room. "It would be a little silly to refuse to let you in now."

"I guess so." Conner was both surprised and relieved to hear the humor in her voice, even if it was slightly bleak.

He turned to look at her as she stepped away from the door. She was wearing a pair of worn jeans and a baggy gray sweatshirt. Her dark hair was pulled back from her face and caught at the nape of her neck with a plain rubber band. There was a smudgy darkness under her eyes that suggested that she hadn't slept any better than he had. She looked worn, softly feminine and damnably young.

"How old are you?" It wasn't the way he'd planned to start their conversation, but then nothing seemed to go quite as it should around her.

"Twenty-two." She looked surprised.

Twenty-two! And he was thirty-seven. He closed his eyes for a moment, his opinion of his own judgment sinking farther still.

"It's well past the age of consent," she said, reading his thoughts.

"I thought you were older."

"Most people do. It's the makeup and the dress. And probably the job." Laura was barely listening to her own explanation. She still hadn't recovered from the shock of his presence. She'd been so sure that he wouldn't come back. "I didn't expect to see you again," she blurted out.

"I said I'd be back." Conner raised his brows as if surprised that she'd doubted his word.

"I didn't think you meant it." She was beyond being tactful.

"You thought I'd just have sex with you and then disappear?"

"Men do it all the time," she said, shrugging.

"I don't. Especially not when the woman in question was a virgin." He made the words almost an accusation.

Laura's chin came up even as color flooded her face. "Do you make a habit of that?"

"Good God, no! You're the first."

"Then I guess it was a first for both of us, wasn't it?" The color in her cheeks belied the sophisticated attitude she was reaching for.

"Why didn't you stop me?" The question had been nagging at him.

"I didn't want to." Laura felt as if her face were on fire, but her chin came up another notch and she met his eyes directly.

"You just decided that I looked like a likely candidate to take your virginity?" he snapped, all his frustration evident in the harsh question.

"Nobody 'took' anything," she flared. "This isn't the Dark Ages. It doesn't mean anything anymore."

She was lying through her teeth. Conner could see it in the way her eyes shifted from his, in the way the color faded from her cheeks.

"So it doesn't mean a thing to you that we slept together?"

She stared at the floor between them and didn't answer. Her arms rested against her midriff, her hands clasping her elbows, her shoulders slightly hunched.

Looking at her, Conner felt a tangled mixture of guilt and anger and tenderness. The guilt he understood. God knows, he had plenty to feel guilty for. The anger was self-directed and he understood that, too. It was the tenderness that bothered him. The urge to pull her into his arms and comfort her was almost overwhelming. It angered him even more. He didn't want to feel anything for her. He didn't want to feel anything for anyone.

"You took one hell of a chance, don't you think? In this day and age, it's criminally stupid to sleep around." The implied accusation was unfair. No one had better reason to know that than he did.

"I don't sleep around," she snapped defensively, jerking her head up to glare at him.

"How the hell do you know that *I* don't sleep around? Did you think about that?" he demanded.

"Did you?" she replied.

It was an unanswerable question. Obviously he hadn't thought about it. He hadn't asked any of the questions that intelligent adults asked these days. All he'd thought about was how good she felt, how desperately he wanted her. It was also obvious that he deserved more blame for that piece of stupidity than she did. He was the one with experience. He sighed and thrust his fingers through his hair.

"No. I didn't think about it." He hadn't thought of much beyond the silken feel of her skin. "In case you're wondering, you don't have anything to worry about."

"Good." The word was strangled.

Conner sighed, sensing that the conversation was excruciating for her, knowing that she wasn't going to find the next topic any more comfortable than the last. He shoved his hands in his pockets, wishing there was someplace they could sit and talk. But the only place to sit was the sofa, and he had no intention of sitting there. Apparently, neither did Laura, because she continued to hover in front of the door. Of course, maybe she was just keeping an escape route open.

"Look, I've got to say it. I didn't use any protection the other night."

"I know," she whispered, hugging her arms closer to her midriff.

"So you could be—"

"I'm not."

"It's too soon to be sure," he continued, determined to see the conversation through to the end. "I—"

"I'm sure." Her voice was stronger, holding a ragged edge of angry embarrassment.

"You're sure?" Conner stared at her, almost afraid to believe that it could be as easy as that.

"I'm positive," she snapped, wishing the floor would simply open up and swallow her. How much clearer could she make it? she wondered, feeling as if her skin might be permanently damaged from the scorching heat that ran up under it. It was stupid to feel embarrassed after the intimacies they'd shared, but she did.

"Thank God." The words were almost a prayer. Some of the tension went out of him.

"If you were so worried about it, why did you come back? I wouldn't have known where to find you." Laura gave him a puzzled look.

Conner wondered just what her experiences with men had been like to lead her to expect him to walk away when there was a chance she was carrying his child. Not that it mattered, he reminded himself. He didn't want to get any more involved with her than he already was. And that was a stupid thing to think. How much more involved *could* he get?

"I couldn't have walked away not knowing," he said.

"Well, now you know."

"Yeah."

She stared at the floor while he looked around the shabby little apartment. The silence grew. Laura stole a quick look at him, wondering why he was lingering. He'd salved his conscience. Why didn't he mouth some polite platitude about being in touch and leave?

"I went to the bar looking for you."

"I don't work there anymore."

"So I was told. There seemed to be some disagreement about your leaving. The bartender said you were fired. One of the waitresses said you quit."

"I guess it was a case of you-can't-fire-me-because-I-quit," she said, shrugging.

"Because of the fight?"

"The owner was a little upset about the amount of damage. And I guess a couple of people are threatening to sue him because they got hurt."

Conner sighed and his mouth twisted in self-disgust. "I guess I should have given it a bit more thought before punching good ole' Randy."

"I'm glad you punched him," Laura said fiercely. "I should have punched him myself. It was time I quit anyway," she added more quietly. *Past time.* She couldn't quite shake the fear that she'd left it too late as it was, that maybe she'd already started down the same path her mother had taken.

She'd had a week to worry about it. Plenty of time to castigate herself for letting loneliness and a few sips of brandy drown out her sense of right and wrong. But now that she was standing here talking to Conner, it was a little harder to feel as she knew she should—that what she'd done had been foolish at best. That feeling that it had been almost destined kept creeping over her, refusing to go away no matter how she scoffed at it.

What did it really matter anyway? It was done. Right or wrong, fate or stupidity, there was no changing what had happened, no sense pretending that she hadn't been changed by it, both physically and emotionally. She brushed a tendril of hair back from her face and looked at Conner, wondering what he was thinking, still faintly surprised that he was here at all.

"I feel bad about you losing your job," he said, when it was obvious that she had nothing more to say about it. "I feel like it was my fault, in a way."

"If it was anyone's fault, it was that jerk's. And I doubt if he's losing any sleep over it."

"Probably not. Still, if I hadn't started the fight, you wouldn't have lost your job."

And he wouldn't have ended up walking her home. He'd have paid for his drinks at the end of the night and left the bar alone, and what had happened afterward wouldn't have happened. Laura wondered if the same thoughts were running through his mind, but she could read nothing from his expression.

"Look, I'd like to offer to help you," Conner said.

"Help me?" Laura didn't want to believe that he was suggesting what she thought he was.

"Jobs aren't lying around on every corner."

"Are you offering me money?" Her tone was so outraged that Conner flushed.

"A loan," he said hastily, realizing what she must be thinking. "If you need it."

"I don't," she said flatly. The truth was, if she didn't find a new job immediately, she didn't have the money to pay her rent. But she'd live on the street before she'd take money from him.

From the look he gave her, she guessed that Conner had a pretty fair idea of the state of her finances. She lifted her chin and met his look, daring him to pursue the subject. Their eyes battled for a moment, his guilt clashing with her pride. He looked away first, deferring to her pride, and Laura allowed her chin to sink a fraction of an inch.

The silence built again, and she wished he would go. She had only to let her gaze slide past him to see the sofa. She'd been doing her best not to think about what had happened between them on that sofa, but it was a little difficult to ignore.

She hunched her shoulders inside the gray sweatshirt and tried to think of something bright and witty to say. What would Miss Manners suggest under these circumstances? Maybe she should write to Dear Abby and ask for advice on carrying on a conversation with a man you barely knew when that man just happened to be your first and only lover.

Just when she was thinking that maybe she should offer him something to drink—and hope that he'd ask for stale cola or milk, because that was about the extent of her offerings—Conner suddenly shifted.

"Well, I guess I'll be going."

"Okay."

This was it. This time, he really wouldn't be coming back. And she had no business feeling all hollow and achy at the thought. He moved to the door and Laura turned to watch him, so many feelings churning inside her that she couldn't grab hold of a single one to know what she was feeling.

His hand on the knob, he turned to look at her. "I'll be in L.A. a couple more weeks. Would you mind if I checked on you every once in a while?"

"I don't need you to check on me."

"Maybe not, but I'd feel better if you'd let me." Something in the set of his chin suggested that he was willing to continue the argument indefinitely.

Feeling breathless and not sure if it was relief or disappointment that caused it, Laura nodded, doing her best to look as if it didn't matter to her one way or another.

"If you'd like."

"I'd like. I'll be seeing you." Conner nodded once and let himself out.

Laura sagged back against the wall, letting her hands drop to her sides now that there was no one but her to see their trembling. Obviously Conner Fox was not much like the men her mother had known. This time she wouldn't take any bets on whether or not he'd be back.

One thing was for damned sure: this trip wasn't turning out anything like he'd expected it would. Conner scowled at the pathetically small stack of applications on the table in his motel room. Jamming his hands in his pockets, he moved to stand at the window that offered an uninspired view of a concrete courtyard and a swimming pool small enough to be considered a bathtub. It was raining for the first time since his arrival two weeks before, but it wasn't the damp weather that made his mood grim.

Two weeks had passed, and still he didn't have the slightest idea who he could hire to replace Mrs. Cuthbert, who was undoubtedly champing at the bit to shake the dust of the ranch from her size nines. The employment agency he'd called before leaving Colorado had done their best, combing their files for likely candidates and setting up interviews.

The candidates had been few and those suitable had been zero. An older woman who looked as if she hadn't smiled since birth. Two women in their twenties, one of whom had backed out when she realized that she wouldn't be able to walk to the nearest mall, the other of whom had made it clear that she wouldn't mind if the job entailed a little extracurricular activity with her employer. A handful of others, none of whom he could imagine sharing his home with.

He shot another irritated glance at the applications. And then there was Laura Halloran. As always, his conscience pinched when he thought of her. He'd been to see her twice more and each time she'd been surprised by his arrival. That surprise annoyed him. That she expected so little from him annoyed him. In fact, there were quite a few things about Laura Halloran that annoyed him.

Like the fact that she'd refused his offer of a loan, lifting her chin—a surprisingly stubborn chin for someone with such gentle features—and looking down that short little nose as if he'd suggested that the money had something to do with the fact that they'd slept together.

And then there was the way she pretended that she had no worries, that she wasn't nearly out of money and options. She hadn't found a new job, and he knew that she'd pretty well run through any money she'd put aside. He could see it in the lines that bracketed her mouth, in the smudgy look around her eyes that said she wasn't sleeping. He'd bit his tongue against the urge to offer her money, knowing she'd only throw it back in his face again.

And why the hell should he care, anyway? Conner scowled more darkly, glaring at the raindrops working their way down the window. He'd slept with her. So what. Did that make him responsible for her for the rest of her life? So she'd been a virgin. Hadn't she said that it didn't matter anymore. She was right. This was the late twentieth century, and a woman's virtue was no longer her only asset. No one cared anymore. He hadn't given a tinker's damn that he hadn't been Rachel's first lover.

But he *had* been Laura's first lover. And he was disgusted to find that he couldn't dismiss it. Primitive and out-of-date as it was, he couldn't shake the feeling that it gave him some kind of responsibility for her. Maybe if he'd believed that she really didn't care... But he couldn't believe it. Her mouth said one thing, but those big blue eyes had said something else completely.

It was those eyes that kept him going back to see her, he thought. She looked at him as if expecting nothing from him, not because of anything he had or hadn't done, but simply because life had taught her to expect nothing. And the fact that she expected nothing made him determined not to give it to her.

From the little she'd said about her past, he'd gathered that her mother had been a less than excellent judge of character when it came to the men in her life. That would account for Laura's low expectations. He had no intention of confirming those expectations.

On the other hand, he couldn't stay in L.A. much longer. He'd left Gun in charge at the ranch and there wasn't a problem that could possibly come up that Gun Larsen couldn't handle. But it wasn't Gun's ranch, it was his and it was past time he was getting back to it.

There were just two problems: Laura Halloran and the fact that he hadn't found a nanny. And one completely insane solution that would solve both problems.

His breath hissed between his teeth as the thought popped into his head. No! He absolutely refused to consider the crazy idea that had come to him in the small hours the night before.

But it could work. The small voice refused to be silenced. It nagged at him.

It couldn't possibly work.

Why not? You've seen her with her neighbor's two children. Remember?

Of course he remembered. He might be insane, but there was nothing wrong with his memory. She'd handled the two kids like a pro and had even said she liked children. But it was still a crazy idea.

You have to have someone to care for the child.

But not this way.

This way would be perfect. You wouldn't have to worry about hiring someone only to have them leave in a few months.

She could still leave.

But she wouldn't. You know she wouldn't. She's the sort who would stick with a commitment once she'd made it.

Conner spun away from the window and glared at the empty room, wishing the little voice in his head was something real and tangible, something he could get his hands on so he could choke it into silence.

"It's crazy." Maybe saying it out loud would get the message through his thick skull.

Why? Because you want her?

"No, dammit!" But it was lie. He *did* want her. He woke up nights, hard and aching with the wanting. No matter how he fought it, he couldn't get the feel of her out of his mind. It was like a fever he couldn't shake.

"Even if she were crazy enough to agree, that doesn't mean she'd have any interest in me," he muttered out loud.

Except he knew that wasn't true, either. He'd seen the awareness in her eyes. She was too inexperienced to hide the sexual curiosity she felt. And though he had no business feeling that way, he wanted to be the one to satisfy that curiosity. For three years, he'd been able to suppress his sexual needs. One night with Laura Halloran and those needs were suddenly screaming for satisfaction.

If she agreed to this totally insane idea, Conner didn't pretend to himself that they wouldn't end up sharing a bed sooner or later. It had nothing to do with what he'd felt for Rachel. It was a purely physical hunger. It was like having an itch that had to be scratched. And he wasn't going to think about the fact that Laura seemed to be the only one he wanted to scratch this particular itch.

He'd been pacing the room with long, restless strides. Now he stopped and stared in the mirror over the bureau. He was going to ask her. There was no sense in pretending that he wasn't. It would be a waste of time to keep arguing with himself.

He turned away from his reflection and strode to the door, snatching up his denim jacket on the way out. Now that the decision had been made, he wanted to act on it.

Crazy as it was, he was going to ask Laura Halloran to marry him.

Chapter 4

Laura opened her refrigerator and studied its contents. If she'd hoped that the carton of milk and half-empty jar of peanut butter might have been transformed into a T-bone steak and chocolate cream pie, she was doomed to disappointment. She stared at the meager contents a moment before shutting the door. If she ate another peanut-butter sandwich, she was going to start talking like Jimmy Carter. Her stomach growled a protest, suggesting that it was not particularly interested in her lingual concerns.

She ignored the complaint, leaning listlessly against the small refrigerator. If she didn't find a job soon, even peanut butter was going to be out of her reach. She hadn't quite reached that point, but the possibility was closer than she liked to think about.

Sighing, she left the kitchen and sat down on the sofa. She stretched her legs out in front of her and studied the bright purple socks that covered her feet. The rain outside matched her mood. Gray and gloomy.

Something had to turn up soon. The statement was less a matter of conviction than one of need. If it didn't... She refused to complete the thought. There were jobs out there. It was just a matter of being in the right place at the right time. She'd only been looking for two weeks. There was no reason to give up—yet.

The problem was, rent was due next week and she didn't have it. Not to mention the small problem of food. She'd made good tips at the bar, but they had simply covered the gap between her paycheck and reality. There'd never been any money to put aside for a rainy day. And, boy, had the rain arrived, in more ways than one.

You could ask Conner for a loan.

Laura winced and closed her eyes, letting her head fall back against the sofa. She'd rather eat worms than ask him for money. She couldn't shake the feeling that it would be all too easy to end up the way her mother had. It had never seemed possible before, but the past couple of weeks had shaken her belief in herself.

But would she really rather end up in the street than ask Conner for a loan?

Opening her eyes, she stared at the drizzle outside, thinking of the street people who'd be huddled in doorways and alleyways, trying to stay dry. She'd always pitied them, but she'd never expected to become one of them. Shivering, she sat up and wrapped her arms around her waist, as if the gesture could warm the sudden inner chill she felt.

Asking Conner might not be an option anyway. He'd be going home soon—his business finished, though she was a little vague as to what that business had been. He'd been to see her twice more since the first time. They'd talked, mostly about impersonal things, surprisingly comfortable talks considering all that had happened between them.

The last visit had been four days ago and he'd said he'd be back just as he had before. But Laura had spent too many years listening to men make promises they didn't keep for her to put much faith in Conner's word. She wouldn't let herself believe in him.

He was probably on his way back to Colorado, determined to forget her as fast as he could. He'd soothed his conscience regarding her, there was no reason for him to think about her anymore, let alone visit again. So even if she could swallow her pride enough to ask him for a loan, it was probably too late.

Sighing, she got to her feet. She'd go through the want ads one more time. Maybe she'd overlooked some possibilities.

An hour later, Laura was still hunched over the paper. She had forced down a peanut-butter sandwich and a glass of milk, finding it difficult to eat despite the fact that her stomach said she was hungry. She'd circled a couple of ads, but she didn't feel particularly hopeful. There didn't seem to be very many people looking for young women with high school diplomas who knew how to wait tables. She was just starting to go over the listings one more time when someone knocked on the door.

Conner. She shot up from the table and then caught herself. She had no business being so excited. If it *was* Conner, then he'd undoubtedly come to tell her he was going home. He wasn't a part of her life and he never would be. She couldn't forget that.

But knowing that didn't seem enough to prevent her hand from trembling when she heard his deep voice through the door. She stopped, drew a deep breath and commanded herself not to be any stupider than she absolutely had to be. When she pulled open the door, she was reasonably sure that she presented a picture of calm friendliness that completely concealed the butterflies tap dancing in her stomach.

"Hi." She backed away from the door to let him in. He brushed by her, bringing the smell of rain in with him.

"Is this a bad time?" he asked, turning to look at her.

"No. Would you like a cup of coffee?"

"Sure." He shrugged out of his jacket and draped it over the back of the chair she'd been using. "I thought it never rained in California."

"You shouldn't believe everything you hear," Laura told him over her shoulder as she ladled the last of her coffee into the filter. Good thing she wasn't a caffeine addict, she thought as she tossed the empty can in the trash.

"Any luck?"

She turned the heat on under the tea kettle and saw Conner frowning down at the paper, folded open to the want ads.

"Not much." She heard the weary sound of her own voice and added quickly, "Something will turn up in the next day or two."

"Probably."

He turned away from the table. Moving to the window, he stared moodily out at the rain for a moment before pacing restlessly over to the table again. Laura watched him, wondering at his mood.

"Did I tell you I have a daughter?" He knew he hadn't told her, of course. He'd told her very little about himself. He turned to look at her, shoving his hands in his pockets, his eyes brooding.

"A daughter?" Laura stared at him, absorbing the implications of this. She felt the color suddenly drain from her face. "You're married?" My God, it was bad enough that she'd slept with him. But if he was married . . .

"No. My wife's dead."

"Oh." It was terrible to feel relieved. As if she were glad the poor woman was dead, which wasn't the case at all. She was just glad that she didn't have to add sleeping with a married man to her list of things to feel guilty about. "I'm sorry," she offered at last.

"Thanks." His tone made it clear that he hadn't mentioned it to get her sympathy.

"How old is your little girl?" Laura asked, when he didn't seem to have anything more to say.

"She's three."

"That's a sweet age."

"Mmm." It could have been agreement or simply acknowledgment.

The kettle began to wheeze, which was all it had been able to manage since she'd dropped it one day and broken the whistle. Laura ignored it for a moment, thinking Conner might have something else to say. But if he did, he was in no hurry.

Just why had he brought up his wife and child now, she wondered as she poured the water over the coffee. She waited a moment to make sure the filter was letting the water drain through into the pot and then set the kettle down. She turned back to Conner, trying to look interested but not too inquisitive.

"Actually, one of the reasons I came to L.A. was to find someone to take over for the nanny I hired a few months back. She wants to go stay with her daughter in the Midwest." He stopped and frowned down at the opened newspaper.

"Have you had any luck?" Laura prompted when he didn't seem inclined to continue.

"No." He dragged the word out as if he were thinking of something else as he spoke.

"That's too bad."

"Yeah." He shot her a quick look from under his lashes and then turned his attention back to the newspaper. Now that he was standing here, the whole idea seemed even crazier than it had back at the motel.

He waited while she lifted the filter cone off the coffeepot and set it in the sink. She'd lost weight. Not a lot, but she hadn't had it to lose to start with. He'd be willing to bet the ranch that there was almost no food in the apartment.

She was wearing another of those baggy sweatshirts that she seemed to favor, and it seemed to dwarf her slender figure. As she reached up to lift two mugs down from an upper shelf, the sweatshirt hem rode up and Conner's eyes lingered on the way her worn jeans molded her bottom. Feeling a familiar response, he dragged his eyes away.

"The ranch is isolated," he said abruptly, taking the mug Laura handed him. "The nearest town is ten miles away, and it's hardly more than a wide spot in the road. There's no running out to rent a video, no cable TV. There's usually a couple of weeks every winter when we're snowed in and the electricity usually goes then. There's neighbors about two miles as the crow flies, a lot farther by road."

Laura listened without comment, her hands wrapped around her coffee mug, her heart beating too fast. Was he going to offer her the job of taking care of his little girl? Why else would he be telling her all this?

She momentarily lost the thread of what he was saying, caught up in an image of herself as nanny to Conner's little girl. She was wearing a black dress and a starched white apron with high button black shoes. A fair-haired little girl with the face of an angel was standing beside her, looking up with an expression of adoration. She'd need an umbrella, of course, one that would carry her over rooftops. Although it didn't sound like there were very many rooftops to be carried over.

She sighed, letting the image go with some regret. She couldn't take it, of course. Too much had happened between them. She wouldn't be able to live in his house and pretend there'd been no intimacy between them.

Unless he didn't *want* to pretend.

Her teeth bit her lower lip. Surely he wouldn't ask her to take care of his little girl so that he could have a convenient bed partner. Did he think she'd be amenable to that sort of arrangement?

"I haven't had much luck getting women to stay on," he was saying. "I don't have time to look for a nanny two or three times a year, and I don't think it's in the best interests of the child for things to keep changing. It'd be best if she had some security, someone she could depend on, someone who'd be around for a while."

It didn't *sound* as if he was looking for a personal playmate. It sounded as if he were genuinely concerned for his daughter's well-being. Laura's heart went out to him, imagining how difficult it must be trying to run a ranch and look after a toddler at the same time.

"I'm comfortably off." He glanced at her and then returned his attention to the coffee he'd yet to taste. "Not rich. Ranching isn't the best way to get rich, but I do fairly well."

He must be trying to tell her that the salary was more than slave wages.

"It's a good life if you don't mind providing your own entertainment. Denver's not so far away that you can't get in for a play once in a while, and there's anything you'd care to name by way of outdoor activities." Having detailed the disadvantages, he seemed to feel that it was only fair to present the brighter side of the picture.

She should stop him now, tell him that it just wasn't possible. No matter how much she needed a job, no matter how reluctant she was to see him walk out of her life, it would be crazy to pretend that she could work for him, live in his house and pretend that nothing had happened between them.

But she didn't stop him. For just a moment, she wanted to indulge in the fantasy that it *wasn't* crazy, that she could accept the job he was about to offer and go to Colorado with him. She'd look after his little girl and make a place in his life. And who knew, maybe someday...

"I know it's a crazy idea...." he continued.

So he saw that much.

"But I think we could make it work. This sort of arrangement used to be pretty common, and people managed to make it work all the time."

What sort of arrangement? Was he talking about having a live-in nanny? True, it wasn't all that commonplace, but it wasn't exactly unheard of, either.

"You don't have to give me an answer now. I'll be in town a couple days more. You can think about it and let me know." He lifted his eyes to hers, and Laura felt her breath catch at the intensity of his look. "I think we could make it work, Laura."

She gave him an uncertain smile, wondering if she'd missed something. He *was* talking about her becoming his daughter's nanny, wasn't he?

"Are you asking me to come to Colorado with you to take care of your little girl, Conner?"

There was a short silence and then: "I'm asking you to marry me."

The words fell into a pool of silence so intense, it was almost a sound. Obviously she was hearing things. It was the only explanation because it wasn't possible that she'd just heard what she'd thought she'd heard.

Conner Fox hadn't just said he wanted to marry her. He had to be joking. But there was no humor in those clear green eyes.

Laura had been leaning against the archway that led into the tiny kitchen, but now she moved to the table and sank into the chair across from where he was standing. Her legs suddenly felt as if she'd just run the L.A. Marathon, weak and shaking. She took a quick, nervous sip of her coffee.

"You're kidding," she said finally.

"No."

She waited, but he didn't add anything to the flat denial. He continued to stand across the table from her, one large hand wrapped around his coffee mug, the thumb of the other hooked in his pocket. He looked completely at ease, as if they were discussing the weather. But the knuckles on the hand holding the cup showed white through his tanned skin.

"Marry you?" She couldn't seem to manage more than two words at a time, but considering the way she was feeling, she was grateful she could get out that much.

"It could work, Laura." He pulled out a chair and sat down, leaning toward her. "Think about it."

As if she could do anything else.

"We hardly know each other." She thought of how well they knew each other, in the biblical sense, anyway, and flushed.

"People used to get married all the time without knowing each other. And they managed to make it work."

"That was a hundred years ago," she protested. "People don't do that kind of thing anymore."

"There's no law against it."

"Of course there isn't. There's no law against believing the moon is made of green cheese, either. That doesn't mean we should believe it." The absurd analogy startled a smile from Conner. Seeing it, Laura felt her own mouth curve. "You know what I mean," she muttered.

"I promise not to insist that you believe anything NASA wouldn't approve of." But the momentary humor faded almost immediately. "I know it sounds strange, but think about it. It would solve a lot of problems for both of us."

"It might also create a few," she pointed out. She'd intended the comment to be sharp and strong, making it clear that the idea was simply too absurd to be considered. But it sounded more as if she were inviting him to persuade her.

"I need someone to take care of the child. You need a job," he said, as if it were an obvious combination.

"A job, yes. You're not talking about a job, though. You're talking about getting ... you know."

"I know. Do you have any prospects of work?"

"No. But something's bound to turn up." Even Laura could hear the lack of conviction in her voice.

"Will it turn up before you end up living in the street?" Now that he'd made up his mind that marrying Laura Halloran was the best way to solve both their problems, Conner was determined to make her see it the way he did.

Hearing him state her fears out loud, Laura shivered. She cradled the coffee mug between her palms—the last cup of coffee she was going to have for a while if she couldn't find work. Or married Conner Fox.

"I don't know," she said finally. "But I can't marry you just because I'm afraid I'll end up in the street."

"Then marry me because the child needs you. I watched you with your neighbor's two little boys last time I was here. You seemed to really like them."

With the instincts of a predator, he'd found her weakness. She adored children. If there'd been a way to do it, she would have gone to college and gotten her degree and become a teacher.

"Your daughter might not even like me."

"She needs some stability in her life," Conner said, ignoring her feeble protest. "She needs someone she can count on being around for more than a few months."

Laura's imagination, obviously in league with him, immediately presented her with an image of a sad-eyed toddler. Did she have her father's coloring or did she take after her dead mother?

"What about her mother? I know your daughter's young, but won't she resent me trying to take her mother's place?"

At the mention of his late wife, Conner's face went very still, his eyes completely without expression. When he spoke, his voice was flat. "She doesn't remember Rachel. You won't have to worry about that."

Rachel. So that was her name. And he still loved her. Laura looked down at the table, her eyes tracing the scratches in the wood. If she'd had any thought that he might be proposing this insane idea because of feelings he had for her, she could give it up now. He was concerned about his daughter—Rachel's daughter—concerned enough to marry a woman he hardly knew.

Marriage. She shivered, hardly able to believe that she was considering the idea. You didn't marry someone because you needed a home. You married them because you loved them, because you wanted to share your life with them.

On the other hand, she'd never met anyone with whom she was even remotely interested in sharing her life. And it wasn't as if men were beating down her door, begging for an opportunity to change her mind. She felt she had a pretty good idea of her attractions, and the list wasn't long. Her mother had been fond of telling her that she was plain and gawky, usually while she patted her own platinum curls and admired the soft pout of her mouth.

As an adolescent, she'd accepted her mother's assessment of her lack of attractions. She'd been painfully shy. As she'd gotten a little older, she'd started to realize that Billie's opinion had less to do with how her daughter looked than it did with not wanting to see her as any kind of competition. Laura had taken a long, hard look in the mirror and decided that she was neither plain nor gawky. Neither was she a beauty, budding or otherwise. She was, at best, quietly pretty. And while looks might not be everything, they went a long way toward attracting the opposite sex.

She'd never really dated and certainly had never had a marriage proposal. Now here was Conner Fox, offering her marriage and a child, all in one breath. And she was actually listening.

"Would this be a real marriage?" She lifted her eyes to his face, trying to judge what he was thinking. "Are you looking for a glorified baby-sitter or do you want a wife?"

Rachel was his wife. Conner squashed the immediate protest and met her eyes.

"I want it to be a real marriage. I think the one thing we can be reasonably sure of is that we're compatible on a physical level."

Without thinking, Laura's eyes went to the sofa. She had a sudden memory of his hands sliding over her skin, the heaviness of his body against hers. No, physical compatibility was not likely to be a problem.

"I won't rush you," Conner said. "We skipped a few steps early on, but we can spend time getting to know each other."

"Most people do that *before* the wedding," she pointed out.

"It's a little difficult when there's a thousand miles between you."

"I guess."

Unable to sit still another minute, she got up and went to stand at the window, staring out at the gray street below. God, she was sick of that view, sick of living in the city, worrying about her safety every time she stepped outside her door. She'd never lived in the country, but the thought of smelling green, growing things instead of car exhaust sounded like heaven. But marriage...

"Couldn't I just come to work for you for a few months and then we'll see how things go?"

"What's the point? The child will still grow fond of you, whether we're married or not. If we're married, we'll both have a vested interested in making it work."

"But what if it doesn't work?"

"It will if we want it to." He made it sound so simple, as if his willpower alone would be enough to make it work. Conner rose and came to stand behind her. Laura didn't turn to look at him, but she was aware of him in every fiber of her body. "Marriage is a gamble, Laura. Even for people who are madly in love, it's a risk."

"But they're at least starting out with something between them," she whispered.

"So are we." He put his hands on her shoulders, turning her to face him. The look in his eyes made her shiver.

Since the night they'd made love, he'd never, by word or glance, suggested that he had any sexual awareness of her. He'd treated her as if she were the sister of a good friend—friendly but slightly impersonal. But there was nothing impersonal in the way he was looking at her now.

In his eyes were all the memories she'd tried so hard to ignore. And if she'd thought he didn't want her, it was obvious that she was wrong. He was making no secret of his hunger. It was in his eyes, those clear green eyes that had haunted her dreams, leaving her flushed and breathless when she woke.

"That's just . . . physical," she got out, trying to sound cool. Hoping he wouldn't release her, because she wasn't at all sure her knees would support her.

"Don't underestimate it. A lot of marriages are based on less."

His thumbs moved restlessly against the soft skin of her upper arms. He wanted her. The thought was both terrifying and exciting. She wasn't the kind of woman who inspired men to lust. To have a man like Conner Fox desire her was a heady sensation. But it also made it difficult to think.

"You said you wouldn't rush me," she said breathlessly.

"I'll give you all the time you want." Sensing that he was a heartbeat away from getting what he wanted, Conner deliberately turned down the sexual heat he'd been broadcasting. He wanted her to agree to marry him, and he was beyond trying to analyze why it was so important to him. "I won't push you into anything."

"Except marrying you." Her voice was tart, but he could feel the way she trembled beneath his touch.

"I can't stay away from the ranch much longer." He didn't like leaving someone else in charge this long, not even Gun Larsen.

"I know." He must be anxious to get back to his daughter. He must love her very much, enough to marry a woman he barely knew to give her a mother. A man who loved his child that much had a lot to give.

She couldn't really be considering his insane proposal, could she? She closed her eyes, shutting out the broad strength of his chest, trying to close out the feel of his hands on her arms, the warm, masculine smell of him. If she said no, he'd leave and she'd never see him again.

No, she wasn't considering his proposal. She'd already made a decision.

"Yes." Her voice was so low, Conner had to lean closer to hear it. Her eyes opened and stared into the ice-green of his. "I'll marry you."

"Good." His hands tightened on her arms, but that was the only sign he gave that he was pleased with her decision. "We need to make some arrangements," he said briskly, stepping away from her.

Laura leaned back against the windowsill, feeling her heart beating much too fast. She felt dizzy. She'd just agreed to marry a man she'd known barely two weeks. With that single "yes" she was acquiring a husband and a stepdaughter. Only time would tell whether it was the smartest thing she'd ever done or a total disaster.

They were married five days later in a tiny chapel in Burbank. Laura wore a simple dress with a full skirt and a scooped neckline. The warm blue echoed the color of her eyes. She'd twisted her mass of brown hair back into a chignon, leaving a few tendrils loose to drift against her neck and forehead. It wasn't exactly a bridal look, but it was feminine.

It wasn't as if Conner were wearing black tie and tails, himself. Since he'd planned on interviewing nannies and looking at horses, he hadn't packed anything suitable for a groom. He wore a pair of freshly pressed jeans and a white dress shirt he'd bought for the occasion. A Western-style string tie completed the outfit. The white shirt emphasized his tan and made his shoulders look even bigger and broader.

Standing next to him, Laura couldn't quite absorb the reality of what was happening. She was marrying this man, a man about whom she knew very little, despite the fact that she'd given him her body. As she listened to the words that were joining their lives together, she couldn't make it seem real.

When the time came, she repeated her vows, surprised to hear the steadiness of her own voice. She was startled when he took her hand to slide the ring in place. She hadn't given any thought to things like rings. The feel of that plain gold band on her finger made everything suddenly very real.

She listened to Conner's whiskey-deep voice as he repeated the vows, but she couldn't lift her eyes from the ring on her finger, the physical symbol of their marriage. Should she have gotten a ring for him? Would he have worn it if she had?

Conner's fingers were under her chin and he tilted her face up to his. The ceremony must be over, she thought, and she hadn't even heard the last of it. They were married. She was married to this man she barely knew with only two strangers to serve as witnesses. But maybe that was appropriate since the bride and groom were little more than strangers to each other.

Conner's eyes seemed to search hers for a moment, and she wondered what he read there. Could he see how nervous she was, how uncertain of this step she'd just taken? Would he care if he did see it? There was no way of knowing whether he saw or cared, but when he lowered his head to kiss her, his mouth was gentle, asking nothing of her. He lifted his head and Laura smiled up at him, her mouth not quite steady, her eyes bright with nervous tears.

"I guess that's it then," she whispered, not sure what she meant, only knowing that she didn't want to let the silence grow.

"That's it." Conner's voice revealed nothing of what he was thinking. She watched him as he thanked the witnesses and the woman who'd performed the ceremony. If he felt any doubts about their bargain, they weren't revealed.

Laura twisted the ring on her finger. For better or worse. Like every bride who'd come before her and

every one who'd come after, she hoped the better
would outweigh the worse.

They started for Colorado immediately. Conner had
picked her up before the ceremony, obviously putting
no credence in the old superstition about not seeing the
bride before the wedding. He'd loaded her things into
his truck, asking only if this was all she wanted to
bring. She'd nodded, finding it easier than trying to
get a word out. Seeing the few boxes in the back of his
truck, it didn't seem like much to show for twenty-two
years of living.

Since Conner had checked out of his motel that
morning, there was no reason not to start their trip
immediately. Nothing except the fact that she was
suddenly terrified of the step she'd taken. But she
could hardly say as much to her new husband.

But terror wasn't enough to keep the turmoil of the
past couple of weeks from catching up with her. She
was asleep before they were outside the city's sprawl.
She woke two hours later, feeling flushed and disheveled
and amazed that she'd slept at all.

It didn't take her long to discover that Conner didn't
mind silences. She asked a few questions about the
ranch, trying to get a picture of it in her mind. He answered
them but he didn't elaborate, didn't give her
any of the details that would have allowed her to flesh
out the rather bare image she had.

He managed the place more or less alone, hiring
help when he needed it. Right now, a man by the name
of Gunner Larsen was taking care of things for him.
Laura immediately pictured a crusty old Swedish gen-

tleman, along the lines of Walter Brennan in that movie where he'd played Frances Farmer's father.

"Didn't he win an Oscar for that?" She wasn't aware that she'd spoken out loud until she caught the startled look Conner threw her. Obviously, he hadn't followed her chain of thought about Gunner Larsen.

"Didn't who win an Oscar for what?"

"Walter Brennan for playing Frances Farmer's dad in *Come and Get It*. Best Actor, maybe?" She frowned, trying to remember.

"Best Supporting Actor," he corrected her. "The first of three, I think."

"*The Westerner* with Gary Cooper."

"He played Judge Roy Bean."

"Ah, but do you remember the name of Gary Cooper's character?" Laura shot him a smug look, sure she had him.

"It was something very Western sounding." He narrowed his eyes and frowned out the windshield at the flat road ahead of them. "Cole Hardin."

She frowned. "Do you know the name of the woman who played the heroine?"

"No. What was it?" He shot her an interested look.

"I don't know," she admitted sheepishly. "I think that was the only movie she ever made."

"A one-hit wonder, I guess."

"Must have been. I didn't know you were a movie buff." This was a whole new side to him, a softer, almost playful side she hadn't expected.

"We don't have cable, but we've got a VCR and plenty of tapes. Rachel was—" He broke off abruptly, his face tightening. Laura saw his fingers clench around the wheel. But when he continued, his voice was carefully even. "Rachel was a movie fanatic. I guess I picked it up from her."

"I used to watch all the old movies on TV. I think I saw every classic film ever made, especially if it had Gary Cooper or Errol Flynn in it. I must have seen *Captain Blood* a hundred times." She was babbling, filling the silence before it could stretch too long, fearing that if she didn't fill it, Rachel would.

On this day, of all days, she didn't want to worry about Conner's first wife. Other than telling her of Rachel's existence, he hadn't mentioned the woman once. Laura hadn't yet decided whether this was something to be grateful for or something to fear. Whichever it was, this was *her* day, not Rachel's. No matter what the circumstances, this was her wedding day and she didn't want to feel that there was a ghost sharing the occasion.

Perhaps her spate of words served their purpose because Conner's hands slowly loosened their death grip on the steering wheel and the tension that knotted his jaw seemed to ease. After a few moments, he picked up the thread of the conversation again, and Laura let her fingers relax from where she'd had them twisted together in her lap.

Talking about old movies carried them through until they stopped for lunch at a truck stop. The food was plain but good and there was plenty of it. Laura didn't have much of an appetite, but she felt very wifely watching Conner eat. When they started out again, the silence between them was more comfortable. They'd made it through their first few hours as a couple.

Laura stared out at the scenery, which was mostly desert, and wondered about the future she was moving toward. What if Conner was wrong? What if Mary resented her? She was only three, but that didn't mean she was going to welcome her new stepmother with open arms. How had her mother died? She hadn't asked and Conner hadn't volunteered that information. Later she'd ask, but not today. One mention of his first wife was enough on their wedding day.

"If the ring doesn't fit, we can have it sized." Conner's words broke into her thoughts, making her realize that she'd been twisting her wedding band around on her finger.

"No, it fits perfectly. I was just thinking about Mary, wondering whether she'll accept me."

"Don't worry about it. You'll be a nice change from Mrs. Cuthbert, who always looks as if she's just run across a very bad smell."

Laura laughed, feeling somewhat reassured. It didn't sound like too difficult an act to follow. She only wished she could say the same about Rachel. Her smile faded. She had the feeling that Conner's first wife had been a very tough act, indeed.

Chapter 5

It was late when Conner pulled into the parking lot of a motel somewhere in Utah. Laura felt as if she'd spent half her life in the truck, staring out at miles of nothing. She was glad Conner's ranch was near the mountains. The desert had a stark beauty of its own, but she couldn't imagine herself growing to love it.

While Conner went into the office to rent their room, Laura slid out of the truck. Standing on the gravel parking lot, she stretched, easing the stiffness from her body. It wasn't until he came back with a key—one key—that it occurred to her that this was her wedding night. Somehow, the ceremony this morning seemed not just miles but years away.

She followed him into the room and then hovered uneasily just inside the door. There were two beds, but she didn't have the slightest idea whether he expected them to use both beds or to share one. What's more, she didn't know how to go about asking him what he had in mind. He'd said he wouldn't rush things. Did their wedding night come under the heading of rushing things?

"You can shower first," he said, setting his carryall on one of the beds. He'd set her overnight bag on the other bed. Did that mean that he *didn't* expect them to share a bed?

When she didn't respond, Conner looked at her over his shoulder. She was hovering in front of the door, as if reluctant to get too far from an exit. Her teeth tugged restlessly at her lower lip as she glanced from one bed to the other. A book wouldn't have been any easier to read than her thoughts.

"I asked for a room with two beds," he said quietly. Her eyes skittered to him.

"You did?" Was that disappointment or relief in her voice?

Conner straightened and turned to face her. "I told you we wouldn't rush things."

"I know. I just wasn't sure what constituted rushing." Her smile was fleeting, revealing more nerves than humor.

"I don't have a schedule."

"It *is* our wedding night," she pointed out, as if feeling it was her duty.

"Do you want to share my bed tonight, Laura?"

He was suddenly standing in front of her, his shoulders blocking out the room. Laura stared up at him, breathless and uncertain. Did she want to share his bed? Just the thought made her dizzy.

"It's our wedding night," she said again, unable to sort out her own feelings enough to give him another answer.

For a moment, Conner considered taking her up on her tacit offer. She was right. This was their wedding night. And he wanted his wife. He'd spent the entire day halfway aroused. Hell, who was he kidding? He'd spent the past two and half weeks in a state of latent arousal.

And now she was his wife and there was nothing to stop him from taking her, from ridding himself of this ache. Nothing except the tired shadows under her eyes and the nearly translucent pallor of her skin. She looked as fragile as a piece of bone china, as if only willpower were keeping her upright. The past few weeks had been rough for her. Her whole life had been wrenched apart and settled into a new pattern—one she must have her doubts about. He'd have to be completely insensitive to ask her to make this a real wedding night.

"We'll wait." Frustration made him sound cool and indifferent, as if he were in no hurry to consummate their marriage.

Inwardly, Laura winced, wondering if she held so little attraction for him that it was no hardship for him to postpone their wedding night. On the other hand, she was so tired, she felt as if she might shatter if he touched her. But it would have been nice if he'd at least wanted to try.

"I'll go take a shower." She stepped around him and went to pick up her overnight case.

"Don't rush." Conner turned to watch her, one hand sliding his cigarettes from his pocket, the other reaching for the doorknob. "I'm going to go to the coffee shop and have a cup of coffee."

"Won't the caffeine keep you up?" Laura frowned at him, concerned.

"It usually doesn't." Who needed caffeine? Spending twenty-four hours a day in a state of semiarousal was enough to give anyone insomnia. "Can I bring you anything? A cup of hot chocolate or something to eat?"

"No, thanks." She gave him a tired smile and reached up to pull the pins from her hair. Conner felt his mouth go dry as it tumbled in a thick, dark mass onto her shoulders. She combed her fingers through it, the movement thrusting her breasts against the fabric of the pale pink T-shirt she'd changed into after the wedding, pairing it with softly worn jeans. His hands tingled with the remembered feel of those soft mounds, the pebbled hardness of her nipples against his palms.

"I'm really beat," she said, stifling a yawn.

He'd been on the verge of stepping toward her, of pulling her into his arms and telling her he'd changed his mind, that they should make this a real wedding night. At her words, he froze, shocked by how easily she aroused him, made him forget his good intentions.

"I'll see you in the morning," he said, his voice raspy. He was gone before Laura had a chance to do more than murmur good night.

She stared at the door, wondering if it was her imagination that made it seem as if he'd fled the room. But she was too tired to think about it long. A hot shower and a soft bed beckoned. It wasn't exactly the wedding night she might have dreamed of, but then neither was anything else about this marriage. Sighing, she dug her nightgown out of her overnight case and headed for the bathroom.

Conner slid onto the red vinyl seat of the booth. The coffee shop seemed identical to coffee shops in Colorado or Arizona or Texas. Red vinyl booths, grayish white linoleum on the floor, a counter with red vinyl stools on chrome pedestals, doughnuts under a plastic dome on the counter and a waitress who looked as if she'd been born to serve burgers and BLTs. He wondered if there was a factory somewhere in Ohio that pumped out coffee shops like this and shipped them all over the country, complete with waitresses and cooks in T-shirts and grease-stained aprons.

He ordered coffee and drew the ashtray closer. He lit a fresh cigarette from the butt of the old one. Now she had him chain-smoking. He stubbed out the butt. A pack usually lasted him close to a week. Since meeting Laura Halloran, he'd been lucky if it lasted a day. Only, it was Laura Fox now.

He reached for the coffee cup as the waitress set it on the table. The coffee was hotter than Hades and strong enough to strip paint. God alone knew how long it had been in the pot, simmering and growing ever more acrid. Conner sipped it appreciatively. It was the first decent cup he'd had since leaving home.

How long would it take her to shower and get to bed? He wanted to get an early start in the morning, but the last thing he wanted to do was run into her coming out of the shower, damp and smelling of soap and woman. His self-control wasn't what he'd have liked it to be, not where she was concerned.

Conner frowned through the thin layer of smoke that rose from his cigarette. He'd always had a healthy sex drive, but he'd never had any trouble controlling it. He'd never felt about a woman the way he felt about Laura—about his wife. From that first night, she'd gotten under his skin, crept into his thoughts and lodged herself firmly in his libido.

One time, he thought, stubbing out his half-smoked cigarette with a quick, annoyed gesture. One time and he couldn't get it out of his head. He lit another cigarette. It hadn't even been the greatest sex he'd ever known. She'd been too inexperienced. He'd been too drunk. It had been quick and powerful, leaving him stunned with the force of it and vaguely frustrated that it hadn't lasted longer. And damned guilty that it had happened at all. He drained the coffee and signaled for another cup. It had never been like that before.

Not even with Rachel.

Guilt stabbed through him, sharp and painful. The skin over his cheekbones tightened and his eyes paled to the color of a glacier. Catching his bleak expression, the waitress gave him an uneasy look as she refilled his cup. Conner didn't even notice her presence.

What the hell was wrong with him? How could he compare Rachel to Laura? The two weren't even remotely alike, not in looks or personality, and certainly he couldn't compare the way he felt about them, in bed or out.

It was just that it had been so long, he thought. That was what had made it seem so incredible. Relieved to have an acceptable explanation, he picked up the coffee cup, biting off a curse when he scalded his tongue on the freshly poured brew. He set the cup down and took a drag off the cigarette, feeling much better.

Obviously, three years was a long time for a man to go without a woman. It wasn't so much that sex with Laura had been extraordinary, it was just that *sex* was extraordinary. So why had his hunger only gotten more powerful? Conner was only momentarily stumped for an answer to that one. A man could fast for days and not feel hunger, but one taste of food was all it took to reawaken his appetite.

He frowned, not entirely comfortable with comparing making love to eating a ham sandwich. But it was the best he had for now, damn it. He lit another cigarette and took a long drag from it. It wasn't until he went to put it in the ashtray that he noticed he had two others already burning there. It occurred to him that he'd never known a ham sandwich to throw him so completely off balance.

He was relieved to see that Laura was already in bed when he let himself in the room a little later. There were two lamps between the beds, and she'd left the one next to his bed on. It cast a shallow pool of light, enough to allow him to negotiate the room, enough for reading in bed if he'd been so inclined and enough to illuminate her sleeping form.

Drawn despite himself, Conner moved to stand between the two beds. Looking down at her, he was struck again by how fragile she looked. She slept on her side, one hand tucked under the pillow, the other lying on top of the covers. With those wide blue eyes closed, she was all pale porcelain skin and tangled dark hair.

One soft curl had fallen across her face, and he reached out to draw it back before it tickled her nose. His hand lingered on her hair. It was like holding a strand of dark silk that curled around his finger like a living thing. It was slightly damp, as if she'd washed it and not taken time to dry it completely before falling into bed. He caught a whiff of soap and shampoo, fresh, clean smells without the slightest erotic overtones.

So why did his gut twist with the need to kiss her awake, to kneel beside the bed and drag her long, slim legs around his hips, to feel her body close around him like a hot, wet glove, drawing him deeper, holding him?

The word he spoke was low and obscene. He pulled his hand away from her hair as if burned. And that just about described how he felt—as if he were on fire. Hunger burned hard and bright in his gut, lapping out to warm his skin all the way to the tips of his fingers.

Abstinence, he reminded himself, a little desperately. Too many years spent alone, too many nights in a bed warmed only by memories that hurt too much to comfort. Abstinence and the knowledge that she was his—his wife, a woman who'd share his home, his bed.

He made himself walk away from her and go into the bathroom. Twenty minutes later, he entered the room again, his hair damp from the shower, a towel wrapped low on his hips. He never slept in pajamas and hadn't thought to buy any—who the hell bought pajamas for their wedding night?—but since he had no doubt he'd be awake long before his new wife was, he wasn't particularly concerned with her being shocked by his sleeping attire or lack thereof.

Lifting the covers, he let the towel drop to the floor and slid between the sheets naked. The bed was more comfortable than any traveler had a right to expect from a motel whose pretensions to class were limited to a reasonable standard of cleanliness, and he sighed as his head sank into the pillow.

It had been one hell of a day. Conner let his body relax back into the mattress and he closed his eyes. After a moment, he opened them and reached for the light switch. His gaze fell on Laura's sleeping figure. She must have felt too warm because she'd pushed the covers down to her waist. The nightgown she wore was perfectly modest. Golden yellow nylon formed a plain bodice with a squared neckline that bared only the upper curves of her breasts. A flutter of ivory colored lace edged the bodice. It was so conservative, it might almost have been considered demure.

Conner felt himself harden in immediate and unwelcome response. Like a randy teenager, he thought, furious with his inability to control the reaction, unreasonably angry with Laura for causing it. Grinding his teeth together, he snapped off the light and lay back against the pillows.

It was a long time before he fell asleep.

Conner suddenly seemed in a hurry to get back to the ranch, Laura thought, watching the scenery rush by. And he didn't seem particularly interested in conversation today. She'd thought that, yesterday, they'd made a reasonable start on their marriage. If it wasn't going to be a relationship built on love—at least not at first—then one based on friendship wasn't half bad. Friendship could lead to other things, including love.

But if Conner had felt the tentative stirrings of friendship, he didn't show much sign of it today. He was polite—she couldn't complain that he was in a bad mood. But a wall seemed to have gone up, with him on one side and her on the other. It was a subtle difference, but she knew it was there. And regretted it.

There was no sense getting paranoid about it, she cautioned herself. It would be foolish to jump to the conclusion that he regretted their marriage. He'd had plenty of time to think about it before the ceremony and nothing had happened since then to change the situation.

More than likely, he was just anxious to get back to his daughter. The explanation soothed her, and she relaxed back in her seat, sure that it was the right one. He'd married her to provide a mother for little Mary. Obviously she meant a great deal to him. Probably since his marriage, he'd made her the focus of his life. And now that he was on his way home, he was anxious to finish the journey so that he could see her again.

The image was highly satisfying. Laura leaned her head against the back of the seat and let herself picture the scene when they got to the ranch. There'd be the ranch house—log, of course, and a big red barn with one of those fancy hex signs painted on the side of it. Or was that in Pennsylvania? She frowned slightly and erased the hex sign.

He'd said he raised quarter horses. She hadn't the faintest idea how a quarter horse differed from a reg-

ular horse, but she put a few graceful horses in the
corral next to the barn. Green pastures stretched behind the house, marked by white fences that gleamed
in the sunlight. Or was that Kentucky she was thinking of? She erased the white fences and replaced them
with picturesque crooked split-rail fences that rolled
over the soft green hills.

There were flower beds beside the house—in bloom
of course, though she hadn't the faintest idea with
what. Roses maybe. Roses were one of the only flowers she could identify so she put a few roses in front of
the house and smiled, satisfied with the way they
looked against the rustic log backdrop.

Coming out of the barn was Gunner, legs bowed
from years in the saddle, limping a little the way Den-
nis Weaver did on reruns of "Gunsmoke." Maybe he
was chewing tobacco. No, that was a disgusting habit.
How about a pipe? She put a pipe in his weathered
hand, but that made him look too much like a sea
captain. Frowning, she abandoned the idea of giving
him an accessory and settled for dressing him in faded
jeans and a red-and-white checked shirt.

Mary was running down the porch steps to greet
them. Her hair was wheat colored, shining in the sun,
with long, golden curls that bounced on her tiny
shoulders. She was wearing a cotton-candy-pink dress
with ruffles at the hem and gleaming white socks with
mirror bright patent-leather Mary Janes. Never mind
that she'd never known a child who could wear an
outfit like that for more than five minutes without
getting it dirty. The image was simply too pretty to
spoil with a realistic smudge.

She'd run to her father, and he would swing her up in his arms, lifting her over his head, his face wreathed in smiles as her childish laughter rang out. He'd hug her close and then turn to introduce her to her new stepmother. Mary would be a little shy, of course, but that would only last a moment. Plump little arms would reach out, anxious to be held. Conner would put his arm around her, drawing her close, and the three of them would stand together, a family.

Laura sighed, feeling tears sting the backs of her eyes at the sweetness of the fantasy. It might not work quite that way, not right away at least. But given time, surely she'd make most of it come true. She dozed off with that thought firmly in mind.

Glancing at her, Conner wondered what she'd been thinking. Frowns and smiles had been flickering across her face like images on a television. Whatever it was, it must have ended on a pleasant note. There was a smile curving her mouth as she dozed. And he was annoyed but no longer surprised by his urge to kiss that smile from her lips, to feel her wake from her dream into passion in his arms.

His mouth flat and grim, he fixed his attention firmly back on the highway. Once he got back to the ranch, things would seem more normal. Rachel had once said that she might have his heart, but the ranch owned his soul and that his happiness depended more on it than on her. He'd told her she was crazy, she'd laughed, and he hadn't given it much more thought.

But on the rare occasions he let himself think about it, he knew it was the ranch that had kept him sane in the months after Rachel's death. He'd clung to its routines and challenges like a drowning man clinging to a spar from a sunken ship. He'd found his sanity there. He was counting on finding his balance now.

It was after dark when they finally drove across the cattle guard, marking the beginning of the road that led to the Rocking D. The ranch had been started by Conner's maternal grandfather and had retained the name he'd given it.

Laura was tired from hours of near-silent travel, as well as tense at the thought of arriving at her new home. She peered out the window, but the only thing she could see was the massive bulk of the Rockies looming up directly in front of them. She tried not to think of the hair-raising descent down out of those mountains. She liked a spectacular view as much as anyone, but she wasn't all that crazy about being right on the edge of that view with nothing but a skinny little guardrail between her and eternity.

If she'd thought that Conner might relax once they got close to home, she was wrong. If anything, his tension seemed to increase with every mile that clicked past on the odometer. Or perhaps it was only her own exhaustion that made it seem as if his body radiated tension. She didn't even want to consider the possibility that he was starting to regret the fact that he was bringing home a wife.

The truck bumped over another cattle guard and under a wooden archway that she guessed probably announced the name of the ranch. Up ahead, she could see the faint glimmer of lights. It occurred to her that she was going to have to get used to the distances out here. She'd lived her whole life in a city where buildings stopped the eye on every side. Looking out and seeing nothing to break the darkness but those few lights made her feel as if the landscape could swallow her whole.

It seemed to take a long time to reach those lights, yet when Conner pulled into the yard and stopped the truck, she had to bite her tongue to hold back the urge to ask him to turn around and keep going. She wasn't ready for this. Whatever had made her think she could do this? It was crazy. *She* was crazy.

"Is...is this it?" It was a stupid question. Obviously this was it. Otherwise why would they have driven for two days to get here? Conner shot her a sideways glance, but he answered as if the question made sense.

"This is it." He reached for the door handle and then hesitated, perhaps sensing some of the terror she felt. "You won't be able to see much tonight. The child's bound to be asleep by now, so you won't have to worry about her until tomorrow."

"Oh." So much for her picture of her stepdaughter flying down the steps to greet them.

Conner waited a moment longer, but he apparently couldn't think of any other reassurance to offer and he pushed open the truck door and stepped down. Laura stayed where she was, not sure whether it was tiredness or nerves that kept her there. She couldn't see enough to make out whether any of it matched her fantasy image. There was certainly a large barn, and she could see the bulk of the house directly in front of the truck. Moonlight gleamed off white paint, banishing the rustic image of log walls.

She jumped and let out a startled little shriek as the door next to her was pulled open. She turned to look at Conner, trying to equate the fact that he was a stranger with the fact that he was her husband. What had she done?

"You plan on sleeping in the truck?" he asked mildly.

"I think I might." There was no disguising the panic she felt, no pretending that, in that instant, she wanted to be back in Los Angeles, even if she had to walk to get there.

"It won't be so scary in the morning," he said, his voice gentler than she'd heard it all day.

His hands closed around her waist, and Laura gripped his shoulders as he lifted her down out of the truck. He held her for a moment, even after her feet were solidly on the ground, and she leaned into his strength. For a moment, she'd looked very alone and very vulnerable. He'd felt that same wave of tenderness that she'd inspired before. He liked it even less than he liked the gut-deep hunger. But he couldn't help reacting to it.

"Least you could do is arrive at a decent hour." Gun's voice preceded him as he pushed open the barn door and stepped into the yard. "You interrupted my beauty sleep."

"It'll take more than sleep to help you," Conner said, releasing Laura to turn and greet his friend and sometime foreman.

Though it was past midnight, he wasn't surprised that Gun was awake. Despite his comment about beauty sleep, Conner had never known anyone who slept less than Gun Larsen. They shook hands and Gun started to speak again, but then his eyes drifted over Conner's shoulder and spotted Laura standing beside the truck, hardly more than a slender shadow against its bulk.

"You brought company?" His brows arched in question as he took in the definitely feminine shape of said company.

"Not exactly." The warmth faded, and Conner's voice took on a certain tension. He turned and reached for Laura's hand, drawing her forward. "Laura, this is Gun, a friend of mine. Gun, this is Laura Fox. My wife."

"Your wife?" It wasn't often that Gun was caught off balance, but he couldn't conceal his shock. He recovered quickly, though, and stepped forward, reaching for Laura's hand. "Pleased to meet you, ma'am."

His back was to the light, making him little more than a shadow looming over her. And *loom* was the operative word. He was at least three inches taller than Conner's six-foot-one-inch frame, and his shoulders looked nearly as broad as the barn behind him. The light that spilled from the barn door caught in hair that was so pale, it seemed to lack color. She had the impression of white teeth as he smiled at her, but his features remained a mystery.

She was tired, nervous and a little frightened. She wanted a shower and a bed, not necessarily in that order, and she'd have preferred to have both of them back in her shabby little apartment in Los Angeles. Defenses down almost rocking on her feet, she said the first thing that came into her head.

"You don't look at all like Walter Brennan," she said, sounding slightly aggrieved.

Gun's brows shot up. He shot a quick look at Conner, but Conner looked as surprised as he felt. "I can't say I've ever given it much thought, but now that you mention it, I have to admit that I've never noticed a resemblance. Is that a problem?''

"No, of course not.'' The moment she'd heard what she'd said, she'd started praying for the ground to simply open up and swallow her. When it didn't oblige, she was left with no choice but to try and pull the tattered shreds of her dignity around her.

"It was just that when Conner mentioned your name, it sounded like...well, it made me think of...'' She let her voice trail off, realizing that there was no way to explain the convoluted rambling of her thoughts without sounding like even more of an idiot than she already did.

"Come and Get It," Conner said, suddenly making the connection.

"Yes.'' She nodded miserably, wishing she were anywhere but where she was.

"Not quite what you pictured,'' he said. A smile tugged at the edges of his mouth.

"I'm sure this all makes sense to you both,'' Gun said, sounding confused.

"Not really,'' Laura admitted. She pushed her hair back from her face, almost swaying with exhaustion.

"You look like you're ready to fall asleep on your feet,'' Conner said. He reached into the back of the truck and pulled out her overnight bag. "Let's get you up to the house. I'll be back in a minute, Gun.''

He set his hand against her lower back, and Laura gave Gun a pleasant, and she hoped sane, smile as Conner urged her toward the house that was now her home. She was too tired to take in much as he pushed open the door and led her inside. There seemed to be a lot of wood paneling and hardwood floors.

"Living room, dining room—we usually eat in the kitchen, which is through there. That door goes to my office. There's a den through here, VCR, television, stereo equipment. The bedrooms are down this hall."

Her head spinning with quick images of large rooms, completely bare of clutter, Laura followed him down the hallway, hearing the muffled thud of his boot heels on the woven runner that carpeted the hall.

"The child's room is there," Conner said, lowering his voice in deference to the sleeping child. "Mrs. Cuthbert is next door."

She would have liked to peek into the room where her new stepdaughter was sleeping, perhaps get a glimpse of the reason he'd married her. But Conner didn't slow his pace. She speeded her steps to catch up with him. Maybe it would be better to wait until morning.

"This is the master bedroom." Laura noticed he didn't refer to it as "our" room, but she didn't let it bother her. It was going to take time to start thinking in plural terms.

She followed him into the room, startled to find herself stepping onto thick carpeting. The room was as big as her older apartment. Of course, she'd seen closets in magazines that were as big as her apartment, she acknowledged ruefully. But this room would have made an extremely generous closet.

There was no wood paneling in here. The walls were plaster, painted a warm ivory shade. The furniture was very Western in style. The bed was made of peeled pine logs, sanded smooth and polished to a dull glow.

The rest of the furniture matched it. The carpet was a soft fawn color, as were the drapes that covered two wide windows. The effect was a wash of soft beiges. It should have been monotonous, but it was deeply restful instead. Had Rachel decorated this room?

"The bathroom's through here," Conner was saying. "Make yourself at home."

"Thank you." Laura sank down on a chair whose thick cushions were patterned in soft Southwestern colors. This was her home now. It didn't feel real. She pushed her hair back wearily.

Conner stood in the middle of the room, perfectly in tune with the Western flavor of his surroundings. From his boots to the Stetson held loosely in one hand, he looked exactly what he was—a Western man. No doubt, Rachel had been a Western woman. Laura felt suddenly very pale and city bred.

"I need to talk to Gun, catch up on what's happened since I left." Conner's pale eyes raked over her, and she wondered if seeing her in these surroundings made him doubt the wisdom of bringing her here.

"I'll just clean up and go to bed," she said, straightening her shoulders and trying to look as if she weren't tired and scared and uncertain.

"Fine." He walked to the door and then hesitated a moment, looking back at her as if he were going to say something else. But whatever it was, he changed his mind. "Good night then."

"Good night." She kept her half smile in place until he'd left, pulling the door shut behind him.

Alone, she let the smile fade and the stiffening go out of her shoulders. She slumped back into the chair and looked around the room, feeling dazed. Her gaze settled on the king-size bed. Had he and Rachel shared that bed? Of course they had. She didn't know her husband well, but she couldn't even begin to imagine him visiting furniture stores to pick out a bedroom set or carefully matching carpets and drapes.

She was so tired, she felt almost sick with it. But she couldn't bring herself to leave the chair and get into that bed. It was foolish and overemotional. What difference did it make if Rachel had slept in that bed? She'd probably sat in this chair, too. But Laura didn't get up.

With a sigh, she leaned her head back against the thick cushions. Tomorrow things would look less frightening. It occurred to her that this was the second night of their marriage. And the second one she was spending alone. A single tear slipped from beneath her lashes.

"I've heard of people bringing back souvenirs when they travel, but don't you think you've gone a little overboard?" Gun grinned as he asked the question.

Conner shot him a look that held both humor and defensiveness. "I didn't need another ashtray with the Hollywood sign on it."

"Well, she's a lot prettier than an ashtray," Gun conceded, watching his friend as he walked the length of the stable, pausing to talk to the stall's occupants. The horses stuck their heads over their stall doors, whiffling soft greetings, seeming to question Conner's absence. "You might have called to warn me," Gun said.

"I might have." Conner scratched behind one chestnut ear, murmuring softly to the animal, reestablishing the bonds of affection.

And that was apparently about all he had to say on the subject of his marriage. Gun's mouth quirked. He'd known Conner long enough to know that he kept his own counsel most of the time. Whatever his reasons for marrying the fragile little brunette he'd brought home, he wasn't going to discuss them now.

"Cuthbert took off about two days after you left," he said, changing the subject.

"She what?" Conner's head jerked toward him, the sudden movement startling the chestnut who snorted his annoyance as he danced back into the stall.

"Said her daughter needed her and packed her things onto her broomstick and flew off." Gun had never made any secrets about his antipathy toward the nanny. The feeling had been amply returned.

"What about the child?"

"I took Mary over to the Williamses'. They were glad to have her. Their kids think she's the best toy they've ever had."

"Thanks." Conner spoke absently, his hand soothing the chestnut's ruffled feelings.

"You think Mary's going to take to having a stepmother?" Gun leaned one shoulder against a post and crossed his arms over his wide chest, his eyes on his friend.

"No reason she shouldn't." Conner shrugged. "She needs a mother, someone who isn't going to quit in six months. Laura's good with children."

"Is that why you married her? To give Mary a mother?" There weren't many men who could have asked that question without running the risk of finding themselves in need of extensive dental work. But Gun had known Conner too long to mince words.

Conner's shoulders stiffened. "My reasons for marrying Laura are my own, but if one of them was to provide a mother for the child, there's nothing wrong with that." His eyes were pale and cold in the dimly lit stable, a look that might have made another man back up a pace.

Gun straightened away from the post and shrugged. "Your reasons are your own," he agreed. "And there's no denying that Mary could use a mother. But there's more to marriage than that. What are you getting from it?"

He didn't expect an answer, which was just as well because Conner didn't have one. At least not one he was comfortable with.

And he still didn't have one when he let himself into the master bedroom an hour later.

He was surprised to see the empty bed. The bathroom door stood open, only darkness beyond. His eyes swept the room, stopping on Laura's slight figure curled in the big chair. She'd drawn her legs up onto the seat, wrapping her arms around her knees and pillowing her head on top of them. She looked like a tired child.

Feeling something stir in his chest, feelings he didn't want to have, Conner crossed the room to her. Bending, he slid his arms around her and lifted her against his chest. She stirred and mumbled something unintelligible and then turned her face against his neck, relaxing in his hold.

He carried her to the bed and pulled the covers down, hampered by the gentle weight of her in his arms. Setting her down on the mattress, he straightened and looked down at her. She stirred things in him he didn't understand. Emotions he didn't want stirred, needs he didn't want to have.

Feeling almost angry, he bent to loosen her clothes, unsnapping the waist of her jeans and sliding the zipper down. The soft wedge of skin revealed made his gut tighten with hunger. He couldn't resist the urge to trail his fingers along the edges of the open zipper, to trace the tiny swatch of lace trimmed pink nylon.

Desire pooled in his gut, dark and powerful, urging him to slide his hands around her slender waist, to taste the shallow indentation of her stomach, to waken her to a passion as strong as his.

With a soft curse, he flipped the covers up over her and spun away from the bed. He hadn't anticipated spending the second night of his marriage the way he'd spent the first—standing under a cold shower.

Chapter 6

Laura was alone when she woke the next morning. The only indication that she hadn't spent the entire night that way was the imprint of Conner's head on the pillow beside hers. She set her hand on that indentation, but there was no trace of warmth remaining. Not that she'd expected it. She knew the day started early on a ranch and from the angle of the sunlight, she guessed it must be halfway to noon.

It struck her suddenly that last night was the first time they'd slept together as husband and wife. Or anything else, for that matter. They'd done no sleeping the night they'd met. And last night, they'd shared a room but not a bed. But now they'd shared a bed, even if it was the bed that had been his first wife's. But the thought didn't bother her as much this morning as it had the night before. Rested, it was easier to accept the fact that Rachel would be a presence in this house.

How could she not be? But she wouldn't be a presence in this bed, not if Laura could help it.

She felt some of her usual optimism return as she swung her legs over the side of the bed and sat up, stretching luxuriously. Marriage had seemed like a good idea in L.A. and all the same reasons were still there. She still wanted a home, a place to build something worthwhile. And there was still a motherless little girl who needed a mother. And Conner? Well, she still wasn't entirely sure what Conner was going to gain from a marriage that he didn't seem all that anxious to consummate. Maybe gaining a mother for his daughter was enough.

Shaking her head, she stood up and headed for the bathroom. She'd worry about the whys and wherefores later. Right now she wanted to shower and dress and go out to see her new home and meet her stepdaughter. No doubt little Mary would be spending the day with her father, making up for the time they'd been apart.

Laura frowned as she turned on the shower. She had to keep in mind that Mary might not want to share her father's attention. The two of them must be very close, and she couldn't expect the child to welcome her into that tight little circle immediately. Well, she had plenty of time.

When she left the bedroom a little later, she was surprised to find the house empty. She'd assumed that Conner would want her to meet his daughter right away. And even if Conner and Mary had gone out, wouldn't the nanny still be here? At least to pack her things?

She peeked into rooms on her way to the kitchen, but she didn't yet feel sure enough of belonging to do more than confirm last night's impressions. The house was large and its rooms were spacious. The decor was Southwestern, done with blond woods and lots of powdery pastels.

It was lovely and restful. But the more she explored, the more she had the odd feeling that no one lived here. The rooms seemed empty in a way that went deeper than merely lacking occupants. It was as if it lacked a heart, a soul. She wondered if it had been different when Rachel was alive. Had she put a sparkle of life into the big rooms?

It was a comforting thought. Laura was frowning as she took a banana from the basket of fruit in the kitchen, feeling as if she were snitching food from someone else's house. It was going to take a while for her to feel as if she belonged here. She quashed the small voice that suggested that the time might never come. Grabbing determinedly for the optimism that had led her to take this crazy chance, she let herself out the front door.

The cardboard boxes that held her things were stacked neatly on the porch. They looked even more pathetic here than they had in L.A. Laura frowned at them as she peeled the banana and took a bite of the sweet fruit. There was something a little embarrassing about having so little to show for her life. On the other hand, if she'd had boxes of fine collectibles and designer clothes to bring, she probably wouldn't have made such a crazy bargain in the first place.

She dismissed her lack of material goods and turned her attention to her surroundings, her new home, she reminded herself. There was no sign of Conner or of a three-year-old. The truck was no longer parked where it had been the night before. She didn't know if that meant Conner was gone or simply that the truck had been put away.

She took another bite out of the banana and surveyed her new home, or as much of it as she could see from the shelter of the porch. The image of green fields and neat split-rail fences required some rapid revision. The land that rolled away from the house was green, but she suspected that would fade as summer approached. The fences were there but they were barbed wire, the taut strands barely visible between the fence posts.

The road they'd come up the night before was dirt. The highway lay somewhere in the distance, out of sight. Other than the fences and the little cluster of buildings around the ranch house, there was no sign of habitation. The land stretched out, empty and wild. It must have looked much the same a hundred years ago and a hundred years before that.

She felt at once intimidated and uplifted by the beauty of it. Drawing a deep breath, she tasted air that held no bite of exhaust, no smell of hot pavement, only the deep, rich scent of growing things. City born and city bred, in that moment, Laura became a country girl.

"Kind of gets to you, doesn't it?" She'd been so absorbed in her first glimpse of her new home that she hadn't heard Gun's approach. Startled, she jumped a little, her pulse accelerating with the small fright as she turned to look at him.

He was standing next to the steps, just about where a flower bed should have been but wasn't. Her first real look at him did nothing to slow her pulse. Gun Larsen was a man who'd make any living female's heart beat a little faster. He was, without a doubt, the most perfect specimen of masculine beauty she'd ever set eyes on. Standing six foot four in his stocking feet and weighing a good two hundred and thirty pounds, he looked as if he should be posing for an advertisement. Any woman would buy anything he cared to sell, whether it was perfume or spark plugs. All it would take would be his picture on the box.

It wasn't just his size or the truly delicious width of his shoulders. He had a face to match the body— broad forehead, eyes of a blue so pure it almost hurt to look at, sharply carved nose, a mouth that made a woman think of long, slow kisses and hot nights, and a jaw that could have graced a Greek coin. His hair was a pale blond that contrasted wonderfully with his tanned skin.

Stunned, Laura dragged her gaze back to his eyes and read the laughter there. She felt her cheeks catch fire as she realized that she'd been staring at him—no, gawking—like a teenager face-to-face with her idol. That she was not the first woman to respond that way was obvious. That he didn't take her response, or himself, seriously was equally obvious.

She swallowed the bite of banana and tried to think of how to salvage the situation. There was no way to pretend that she hadn't been staring at him, nothing to do but brazen it out.

"I was right. You don't look a thing like Walter Brennan."

"Thank you for that." His smile revealed a set of perfect teeth that gleamed white against his tan. He didn't seem to have any of the arrogance, the self-awareness that often went along with such physical beauty.

Swallowing hard, Laura remembered the half-eaten banana in her hand and took another bite of it, feeling her pulse slow to normal. It was just the first shock of seeing so much male beauty first thing in the morning that had thrown her. Her reaction to Gun held none of the gut-deep impact of the way Conner made her feel.

"Conner asked me to let you know that he's gone over to the Williamses' to pick up Mary," Gun said, as if reading her thoughts.

"The Williamses'?"

"Nearest neighbors. They live over yonder." He nodded his head to the north. At least, she thought it was north. "Not all that far if you're a crow or on horseback, but it's a bit of a drive."

"Did Mrs. Cuthbert take her over there?"

"Nope." Gun tilted his head back on his forehead and looked up at her. "Cuthbert took off right after Conner left. I figured I couldn't handle the ranch and take care of the little one, so I took her over to Cy and Dottie's. They've got three of their own and they all think Mary walks on water. I'd guess they've done a fair job of spoiling her rotten by now."

He didn't seem concerned, but Laura frowned as she swallowed the last of the banana and began folding the skin. It wasn't going to make it any easier to establish herself with her new stepdaughter if Mary had just spent the past three weeks having her every wish indulged.

"You planning on putting a bow on that and mailing it?" Gun's question made her realize that she'd been folding the empty banana skin into precise layers, creasing the skin with her thumbnail so that it would lie flat.

"I guess not." She shook her head and looked around for a place to dispose of the abused peel.

"There's a compost pit around back by the garden." Gun said." I could show you around a bit 'til Conner gets back." Laura hesitated only a moment before nodding. She didn't know how long it would be before Conner and Mary returned, and she wasn't all that anxious to return to the empty house.

Over the course of the next half hour, Laura and Gun established the beginnings of a comfortable friendship. Once she'd recovered from the shock of his remarkable looks, Laura found herself almost forgetting them. Mainly because Gun himself seemed to put no stock in them.

He took her on a brief tour of the ranch, starting with the huge kitchen garden behind the house. Laura, who'd never had a place to cultivate more than a houseplant or two, found her hands itching to dig in the rich black soil.

"Conner takes care of the garden, more or less. Dottie and her oldest girl usually can the harvest in exchange for half the produce," Gun told her, sensing her interest. "They don't have a whole lot of flat land around their house and what they do have, Cy's planted roses. They run a few cattle, but they're not real serious about it. Cy makes a fair living dabbling with a paintbrush and Dottie writes children's books. It's a good thing, too, because their place is mostly mountain. They had to import a special breed of cattle from Scotland.''

"Because of the altitude?" Laura asked.

"Nope. These cattle are bred to have shorter legs on one side so they can stand upright on a slope. Regular cattle just tumble right off.''

Laura blinked at him, trying to picture cattle like he'd described. It didn't make sense, and she opened her mouth to say as much when she caught a glimpse of the wicked laughter in his eyes.

"What happens if these cattle should stumble onto a level area?"

"They fall over," he answered promptly.

"I think you're pulling my leg," she said primly.

"Me?" He put his hand over his heart and looked the picture of hurt innocence.

Besides the barn, there were stables and several outbuildings that served as storage for everything from equipment to spare parts to grain. It was Gun who introduced her to the horses and explained that a large part of the ranch's operations was the training of them. Her husband was apparently well-known for his ability to train a fine cutting horse. Laura immediately had an image of a horse with a knife gripped between its teeth, but Gun explained that a cutting horse was one who could cut a particular animal out of a herd. A well-trained cutting horse became an extension of its rider's brain, responding to signals almost before they were given.

Laura felt a wifely pride at the thought that people from all over the Western states came to Conner to train their animals as well as to buy the horses he raised. She didn't know anything about horses, cutting or otherwise, but Gun did and there was no mistaking his admiration for Conner's skills.

She was sitting on the seat of the tractor, listening to what she suspected was a highly exaggerated story of Gun's encounter with a mountain lion, when she heard the sound of Conner's truck coming up the road. Her head jerked up, her eyes fastening on the blue vehicle through the cloud of dust it was kicking up.

Seeing he'd lost her attention, Gun glanced over his shoulder before reaching up to put his hands around her waist and lift her off the high seat. When Conner had held her the same way to lift her down from the truck, Laura had felt her pulse start to race and breathing had suddenly taken a conscious effort. She hardly noticed that Gun was touching her, though her hands rested lightly on his shoulders for balance as he lowered her to the ground.

That was how Conner saw them as he stopped the truck in the yard. Gun's big hands nearly circling Laura's waist, sunlight glinting off his pale gold hair as he lifted her down and Laura smiling at him as he set her on her feet. He felt a sharp twinge of something that could have been—but wasn't—jealousy.

He knew better than to be jealous of Gun. Given the time and place Gun was hell on wheels where women were concerned, but he'd never look at another man's wife. Besides, to be jealous, Conner would have to be emotionally involved with Laura, and he wasn't. He was married to her, but that wasn't emotional involvement. So he must have a touch of heartburn from gulping coffee for breakfast. That would explain that twinge in his chest.

Laura stood a few yards from the truck, linking her fingers together to still their nervous trembling. She wasn't sure what made her more nervous—seeing Conner on his home ground or meeting his daughter.

Conner got out of the truck and nodded in her direction, apparently all the greeting he felt was necessary. He walked around the front of the cab to open the passenger door. He was wearing a pair of worn jeans that clung lovingly to his hips and a blue chambray shirt that had seen so many washings and spent so much time in the sun that it had faded to a pale, dusty blue. A gray Stetson covered his head, as natural a part of his working attire as the narrow black boots he wore.

He reached into the cab to lift out his daughter, and Laura felt her breath almost stop. Sensing her fear, Gun touched her shoulder.

"Mary's an easygoing little tyke. Don't you worry about her taking to you."

"Thanks." Laura forced her feet to move, walking toward Conner as he lifted his daughter out of the truck and set her on the ground, giving Laura her first look at the child she hoped would come to think of her as a mother.

Mary was not the golden-haired little girl of Laura's fantasy. Her hair was a dark russet shade that held hints of fire where the sunlight caught in it. The pink ruffled dress and white ankle socks had become a pair of denim overalls and dirty sneakers. Her face was sweet without being exactly pretty.

Laura had expected her to cling to Conner's side, reluctant to leave him and perhaps shy about meeting a stranger. She stayed where she was, not wanting to advance too quickly and seem pushy. She waited for Conner to introduce his new wife to his daughter.

But before Conner could say anything, Mary glanced past Laura. Seeing Gun, her small face suddenly broke into a smile that displayed a set of perfect, tiny white teeth.

"Unca Gun! Unca Gun!" She darted away from her father, her short legs moving as fast as they could over the dusty ground as she hurled herself toward the big man.

"Muffin!"

Laura stepped back and watched as Gun crouched down to meet the little girl's charge. His big hands caught her under the arms as he rose and tossed her over his head. She shrieked with laughter, her tiny fingers reaching for his hat as he held her above him and bounced her.

Laura glanced from the charming scene to Conner, wondering if Mary's obvious enthusiasm for Gun bothered him. The brim of his hat shadowed his face and it was impossible to make out more than the pale glitter of his eyes, but he didn't seem at all disturbed that his daughter had shown no hesitation at abandoning the father she hadn't seen in three weeks for the company of her adoptive uncle.

As Conner moved toward the little group, Laura filed the thought away for later examination. By the time Conner reached them, Mary was settled on Gun's hip, his hat perched comically on her head and falling down over her eyes. Conner left her where she was while he made the introductions.

"This is Laura. She and I are married. She's going to live with us from now on and look after you." As introductions went, Laura supposed it was all right. It wasn't exactly effusive, but then a low-key approach was probably the safest idea.

Gun had tilted his hat back on Mary's head, and she regarded Laura from under its shelter, her eyes solemn but unafraid. Conner's eyes, Laura saw, and felt her breath catch at the resemblance.

"Hello, Mary. I hope we're going to be friends."

"H'lo." Mary was willing to return the greeting but seemed to be withholding judgment on the friendship angle. Which was as much as she could have hoped for, Laura thought.

"Are you hungry?" she asked, knowing that it must be approaching noon. "I could make us some lunch. All of us," she added, lest Mary get the idea that she was trying to steal her away from the men.

Mary ducked her head, as if unwilling to commit to lunch. Conner said nothing, only watched the proceedings with those ice-green eyes that revealed nothing of what he was thinking. It was left to Gun to respond.

"I'm starving. And I can hear someone's tummy growling." He lifted Mary higher and put his ear against her tummy. "Yup, I thought so. Your tummy says it's time to eat." Mary giggled and pulled his hat down over her eyes again.

"Well, I guess I'd better go see what there is to eat," Laura said, hoping that there'd be something in the kitchen that she could throw together. She tried to look confident as she walked toward the house and hoped no one would notice that she had to wipe her damp palms on the legs of her jeans.

By the end of the day she was so tired, she felt as if she'd run a marathon while carrying a ten-pound weight in each hand. Lunch had gone off better than she'd hoped, largely thanks to Gun's support. Conner had contributed little, hardly seeming aware of her, though several times she'd caught him watching her with an enigmatic expression she couldn't even begin to read.

When the meal ended, Mary consented to stay with Laura while the two men went outside to work. Once she'd gotten over her initial shyness, Mary proved to be friendlier than Laura had dared to hope. She doubted if the child understood the difference between her father bringing home a wife and his hiring a replacement for the departed and seemingly unlamented Mrs. Cuthbert.

From what Conner had said about the difficulties of retaining help, perhaps Mary was simply so accustomed to new nannies turning up in her life periodically that she accepted them without a fuss. Laura didn't mind if the child saw her as a new nanny. She was certainly more that than wife.

She put Mary down for a nap after lunch and ventured into the master bedroom again. Conner had carried the boxes that held her clothes in from the porch. Putting them away seemed as good a task as any, and maybe it would help to make her feel as if she really lived here.

Pulling open the closet doors with a defiant flourish, Laura nearly sagged with relief when she saw nothing but a modest row of men's shirts and a suit. She hadn't realized until that moment just how afraid she'd been that she was going to find Rachel's clothes still in possession of the closets and drawers. Just as she feared that the other woman's spirit still occupied a large portion of Conner's heart.

But she wasn't going to worry about that right now. Today was for laying the groundwork for her future relationship with her stepdaughter. That was why Conner had married her, after all.

Dinner was a repeat of lunch, with Gun and Laura carrying most of the conversation. Conner seemed to have little to say, and Laura caught Gun throwing him puzzled glances, as if wondering at his taciturnity.

After dinner, both men disappeared outside while Laura did the dishes. So far, the big kitchen was the only room that was starting to feel like it could be hers. Maybe it was that she'd always loved to cook. Maybe it was just that the room didn't seem to speak as much of another woman's taste as the rest of the house did. Whatever it was, she felt something approaching contentment as she rinsed the plates and loaded them into the dishwasher while Mary drew pictures at the table.

She could make a home here, she knew she could. Given time and a little encouragement, she could banish the emptiness from the house, make the rooms alive again. Shutting the dishwasher and flicking the lever to turn it on, she frowned in the direction of the front door, the one through which her husband had vanished. The time she'd have. Conner had made it clear that he considered this marriage a long-term commitment and she knew him well enough to know he'd meant it. The encouragement . . . well, that she wasn't so sure about. Was Conner going to encourage her or ignore her?

Sighing, she straightened away from the counter and crossed to the table to admire Mary's artwork before suggesting that it was time to get ready for bed.

Supervising the little girl's bath and getting her into her nightgown, Laura felt all her uncertainties fading away. This was what she'd always wanted, a home, a child to love. Real, lasting things, not the ephemeral promises her mother had spent her life grasping at, finding them always out of reach.

And when she tucked the little girl in and Mary solemnly requested that she kiss her doll good night, Laura's heart fell into her tiny hands, never to be recaptured. Tears stung her eyes as she bent and kissed the grubby cloth face. She understood, more than she ever had before, Conner's willingness to do what he had to to provide his daughter with the stability she needed. Surely the fact that he loved his daughter so deeply was a hopeful sign. A man capable of that kind of love was worth struggling to understand.

She read Mary a story, wondering if Conner would come in to kiss his daughter good night. But there was no sign of him when the story was finished, and Mary didn't seem to be expecting him. So Laura turned off the lamp, leaving a pink elephant-shaped night-light to chase away the dark shadows, and left the room.

She hesitated in the hallway. Maybe she should go see if Conner had come in while she was occupied with Mary. But if he had, he certainly knew where he could find her. She let herself into the master bedroom, but wasn't surprised to find it empty. Somehow she'd had the feeling that tonight was going to be like the night before.

Maybe Conner was just giving her a chance to settle in, she told herself as she took her nightgown into the bathroom with her. Or maybe he didn't want her. She stared at her reflection in the mirror but found no answer to her questions.

Chapter 7

Nothing was what she'd expected.

Laura carefully sifted a layer of soil over the carrot seeds she'd just planted. Going back along the row, she tamped the soil down with the back of the hoe. At the end of the row, she stopped to rest a moment.

It was so quiet, she could hear a horse stamp in the corral next to the barn and the sound of a hammer striking metal as either Conner or Gun repaired some piece of equipment in the barn. Closer by, she could hear Mary murmuring to her doll as the two of them played at planting their own garden.

As her eyes settled on the little girl, Laura's mouth curved in a smile. The one thing that was exactly as she'd expected—hoped—was Mary. In two short weeks, she'd grown to love the little girl as if she were her own, and she didn't think she was wrong to believe that Mary was starting to reciprocate those feelings.

While "Unca Gun" was still her prime favorite, Mary was starting to turn to Laura more and more, not just for the care she would have expected from her nanny but for the love and affection every child needed. And Laura was more than ready to give her that affection. She couldn't imagine *not* loving such a sweet little girl.

Her smile faded, her eyes going past Mary to the corral. Conner was working one of the young horses, walking it on a rope. Though she couldn't hear it from here, Laura knew he'd be talking to the animal, murmuring to it, hypnotizing it with the sound of his voice, teaching it to trust him. He had endless patience with the horses. He spent every minute with them.

Or maybe it was that he was spending time *away* from her and Mary and the horses provided him with a good excuse. She folded her hands over the top of the hoe and angled it until she could prop her chin on her hands. She'd assumed that Conner must love his daughter a great deal if he was willing to marry a stranger to provide her with a stable home. She'd envisioned cozy little scenes of the two of them: Mary cuddled on his lap while Conner read her a story, Conner sweeping her up in his arms to hug her close, that enigmatic expression erased by affection.

But in the time she'd been here, he hardly seemed to know he had a daughter. And from Mary's acceptance of the situation, it seemed clear that it was all she knew. So if it wasn't devotion to his daughter that had led him to suggest marriage, what was it? Maybe he had just figured she'd be more likely to stick around if they were married, saving him the trouble of having to find someone new to care for the child he didn't seem to want.

Or maybe he'd felt so guilty about making love to her that he'd felt obliged to marry her. If that was the case, he didn't seem in any hurry to repeat the crime now that it was all legal and sanctioned.

She sighed again, her eyes taking on a wistful look. Two weeks and he hadn't so much as kissed her. At first, she'd been grateful for the chance to find her feet without the added pressure of sharing a bed with him. But she had to admit that she was starting to feel just a little piqued by his lack of interest. He'd said he wouldn't rush her, but she was starting to think that the promise hadn't caused him any real hardship.

Conner glanced away from the colt he was walking, his gaze settling on the slim figure of his wife. She was standing at one end of the vegetable garden, leaning on the hoe to take a break. The child was playing a few feet away from her, digging in the dirt with a stick, the rag doll an ever-present companion.

It seemed he'd made a good choice in finding someone to mother her. She'd taken to Laura as if she'd known her all her short life. And Laura had the patience of a saint in dealing with her. She didn't seem to mind mud-streaked clothes any more than she minded the endless stream of chatter—much of it unintelligible.

Watching her with the child, Conner sometimes felt the old lonelinesss reach up to grab him by the throat. He wondered what it would be like to let down the walls, to let himself be drawn into the small circle of warmth Laura was creating. He shoved the thought away, reminding himself of the terrible price that came with letting down the walls. He didn't ever want to be that vulnerable again. It was too great a risk.

Laura leaned over to look at something Mary was showing her, and Conner felt his mouth go dry. The jeans she wore molded her bottom with loving care and clung to the length of her legs. No woman her size had a right to have legs that long. The kind of legs made to wrap around a man's waist.

She straightened, and he caught the sound of her laughter on the breeze. His eyes drifted from her smiling face to the proud thrust of her breasts against the pale yellow T-shirt she wore. It wasn't possible at this distance, but he could almost imagine that he saw the little peaks of her nipples pushing against the knit fabric. If he were standing beside her, he could slide his hands under her T-shirt and feel her belly quiver under his touch. He'd move his hand upward and—

"Damn it!" The colt, bored with Conner's lack of attention, had moved to stand right behind him and butted Conner in the back with his head, nearly knocking him off his feet.

Exasperated, his fantasy shattered, Conner turned, hearing the rich sound of Gun's laughter. He threw a glare in the direction of the other man who leaned against the fence. From the look on Gun's face, he had a fairly clear idea of where Conner's thoughts had been. The idea did nothing to improve his mood. Not that his mood had been particularly good to start with. Sexual frustration did not put a man in the best of moods.

He led the colt back into the barn and put him in his stall. Picking up the brush, he began stroking it over the young animal's back, praising him for his efforts in the corral. But for once, his thoughts weren't on his work.

He should have slept with her that night in the motel. That had been his first mistake. He'd compounded it by not sleeping with her the first night here. He'd told himself that he was just being considerate, keeping his promise not to rush her. But the truth was that he'd been trying to prove something to himself.

From the moment he'd seen her in that dingy bar, he'd wanted Laura Halloran. The hunger had burned in him and he'd used the whiskey as an excuse to give in to it that night in her apartment. But it hadn't been enough. The next time he saw her, he'd realized that the hunger was still there, just as hot and aching as it had been before.

He hadn't spent so much time thinking about sex since he was a teenager. And not just any sex, but sex with his wife. Long, slow sex that left them both drugged with pleasure. Fast, hard sex that left them panting and breathless. Any way, anywhere as long as she was his. He was damned near obsessed with the thought of having her.

And he resented it bitterly. He didn't like knowing that she could sneak past his control the way she had; that he couldn't simply put her out of his mind. His concentration was shot to hell. His temper was on the wrong side of rabid. He'd taken to sleeping on the sofa in his den because he couldn't stand the torture of sharing a bed with her. And since five feet of sofa was not the best accommodation for six feet of man, his nights had been restless for more reasons than one.

It might not have been so bad if he'd thought that the situation bothered her at all. But she seemed quite content to leave things as they were. She was keeping her end of the bargain, doing what he'd asked, making a home for the child.

He couldn't put his finger on just what the change was, but the house seemed different these days. The fine layer of dust that had coated the furniture in most of the rooms was gone, but it was more than just a lack of dust. Laura had thrown open curtains and let the sun stream into the room. And set on tables were bunches of early wildflowers stuffed carelessly into vases and water glasses.

It was as if the house had been asleep and Laura had come along to wake it up, to shake out the dust both literally and figuratively. There were hot meals on the table each night and conversation, though it was mostly between her and Gun.

She was real friendly with Gun. Conner scowled over the colt's back at the wooden side of the stall. Gun usually moved on sometime before the middle of summer, and for once Conner would be glad to see him go.

Conner put away the currycomb and gave the colt one last pat before pushing open the stall door. He didn't know what he was going to do about the situation, but he knew it couldn't last indefinitely. He was starting to think that all the snowmelt in the Rockies wouldn't provide a shower long enough and cold enough to drown the fire in him.

* * *

Laura tilted her face upward, letting the warm spray wash over her. The muscles in her shoulders ached from the work she'd done in the garden. But it was a good ache, one that came with a satisfying feeling of having accomplished something worthwhile. Her legs had often ached after a night of serving drinks, but she'd never felt good about it.

She reached out to shut off the water. She was content with her choice on so many levels. The house, the land, Mary—they were all so much more than her fantasies. If only Conner would open up to her. Heck, if he'd just stay in the house and talk to her, she thought ruefully. He'd disappeared right after dinner again. She suspected he was sleeping in the den because after the first couple of nights he hadn't shared the big bed with her.

Sighing, she pulled open the shower door and reached for one of the thick white towels that hung on the rack. Things would be just about perfect if only her marriage were a real one.

Laura had just snagged the towel and was shaking it out so that she could wrap it around herself when she heard a soft click and cool air brushed over her damp body. Startled, she jerked her eyes toward the door, where they collided with her husband's cool green gaze.

For the space of several heartbeats, they were both frozen. Conner stared at her, seeing his fantasies come to life. Her skin was flushed from the warmth of the shower and still damp. Her hair was pulled on top of her head in one of those soft buns that always made a man's fingers itch to pull the pins loose. Soft tendrils lay against the column of her neck, their darkness contrasting with the ivory of her skin.

The firm mounds of her breasts and the dusky aureole that surrounded her nipples seemed to beg for the touch of his mouth. Her waist was narrow, flaring out into the soft curves of her hips. The triangle of curling hair at the top of her thighs tantalized even as it concealed her womanly secrets. And then there was the slender length of her legs, those impossibly long legs that had haunted his dreams.

Laura recovered from the frozen moment of shock and started to wrap the towel around her, not sure her shaking hands were up to the task. But then Conner's eyes swept to her face. How could she have ever thought his eyes were like ice? They were fire, a pale green flame that seared her, weakening her knees, starting an ache deep inside her.

"I thought you were still with the child." Conner's voice was a low rasp.

"N-no." He reached for the buttons on his shirt, and Laura's fingers went lax. The towel dropped to the floor. "She . . . she's already asleep."

"Good." He stripped the shirt off his shoulders, baring a chest muscled from years of hard work and tanned from the sun. Dark blond curls dusted his skin, tapering to a narrow line that slashed across his taut stomach to disappear beneath his belt—the belt he was unfastening.

"Oh." Laura grabbed for the edge of the shower door to keep herself from melting into a heap on the tile. He hadn't touched her, but her breathing was already ragged.

The rasp of his zipper made her mouth go dry, and she closed her eyes when he put his hands on his hips and started to shove the worn denim down and off. But she opened them almost immediately. Conner kicked the jeans out of the way and started toward her. She'd thought he didn't want her, but it was obvious that she'd been wrong. The evidence of his desire stood out from his thighs, tumescent with need.

She'd half expected his arms to come around her and carry her to the rug at her feet. The look on his face said that his need was that powerful. But he stopped inches away from her. He said nothing, only looked at her, his eyes burning with hunger, demanding an answer to questions unvoiced.

Unable to sustain the force of that look, she lowered her eyes and found her gaze caught by the rigid length of him. Caught and held. She knew the feel of him, had taken him into her body, felt him in the deepest, most intimate part of her. Yet this was the first time she'd looked at him, seen him.

Hardly aware of her action, she reached out, touching him with trembling fingers, feeling the velvet softness that sheathed steel hardness. And in so doing she answered the question he hadn't voiced.

His hands came up to cup her breasts, callused thumbs dragging across the sensitive peaks. Laura trembled, feeling the light touch all the way to her toes.

She was everything he'd remembered, everything he'd dreamed. Water beaded her skin, an invitation he couldn't resist. He bent, sipping the moisture from the slope of her breast, feeling her tremble. And when he opened his mouth and took her inside, she whimpered low in her throat, her hands clinging to his shoulders as her knees gave up the struggle to keep her upright.

Conner's arms were there to catch her, one sliding beneath the gentle swell of her bottom, the other an iron band across her back as he lifted her out of the shower. He held her so that her breasts were level with his mouth, ravishing the soft flesh with teeth and tongue until she cried out with need, twisting against him.

He wanted to take her where they stood, her legs around his waist, his back to the tiled wall. But not this time. He wanted her too much, his hunger was too overwhelming for that kind of control. He let her slide down the length of his body, torturing them both, fanning the fire that burned between them.

As Laura's feet touched the rug, his mouth caught hers in a ravening kiss, his tongue thrusting boldly into her mouth in an unmistakable rhythm. Trembling, dazed by the abrupt explosion of passion, Laura clung to him, feeling as if she'd been swept up in a whirl-wind.

Conner's hands cupped her bottom, lifting her until his manhood was cradled against the soft thatch of hair at the top of her thighs. Laura whimpered, her head falling back, exposing the delicate arch of her neck to his hungry mouth.

She wasn't even aware that they were moving until she felt herself falling. Before she had time to be frightened, the bed came up beneath her. Conner loomed over her, his broad shoulders blocking out the light, his pale eyes fever-bright with a hunger that half frightened her.

"The sheets," she whispered, hardly aware of what she was saying but feeling a sudden, deeply feminine uncertainty. "I'll get them wet."

"To hell with the sheets."

He took her mouth with his as his thigh parted her legs. He caught her startled cry as his hand cupped her mound, claiming it as his own. He parted the soft folds, groaning as he felt the heat and moisture that told him her hunger burned almost as hot as his.

A memory haunted him—that of her cry of pain when he'd first taken her, the knowledge that she hadn't been ready for his possession, the fact that the final fulfillment had been his alone. Determined that this time would not be like the first, Conner eased one finger inside her, testing her readiness for him even as he gave her pleasure.

Laura cried out, her hips lifting off the bed, her thighs opening to him as he deepened the touch, his callused thumb brushing gently over that most sensitive part of her. Hearing the plea in her voice, feeling her readiness in the honeyed response of her body, he knew he couldn't wait another instant to complete their union.

He rose above her, using his knees to open her to him. Laura's lashes lifted as she felt the velvet-and-steel pressure of him. He eased forward and she felt her body yielding to his, surrendering in an age-old way. His eyes locked on hers. He caught her hands in his, pressing them back against the pillow on either side of her head, holding her a willing captive. He lowered his head, his lips settling on hers as he completed their union with a heavy thrust that carried him deep inside her.

If she could have, she would have cried out, not in pain, for there was no pain, although the very intensity of his possession hovered on the knife edge of pain. Her hands fisted in his, her body arching against him as if undecided whether to take him deeper or throw him off. But the answer was in the way she lifted her legs against his hips, in the instinctive need to feel him in her very soul.

Conner released her hands but only to wind his fingers in her hair. She felt the pull against her scalp as the pins tugged loose and then her hair was spilling into his hands and over the pillows, chocolate silk against the smooth white linens.

"I've dreamed of you like this," he said, his voice a guttural whisper.

There was no chance to answer, to tell him that he'd been part of her dreams, too. He was easing away from her and Laura whimpered a protest, her hand coming up to clutch at his waist, afraid that he was going to leave her.

His smile was pure, masculine triumph as he felt her hold him, sensed her frantic need. Laura felt a spurt of rage and struggled against him, against her own need. Then he surged forward, sheathing himself in her and she cried out, a high, keening sound of pleasure that ran straight down his spine, exploding at its base.

And suddenly there was no time for games, no matter how pleasurable. He'd thought to draw this first time out, to make it last all night, but that wasn't possible for either of them. If he'd hungered, so had she. If he burned, she was the flame. It was rougher than he'd intended, an elemental coming together that he could neither deny nor control.

And when the final explosion came, she was with him, her short nails biting into his back, her slender body arching taut as a bow string under him. She cried out in startled wonder as the light of a thousand stars seemed to burst inside her, dazzling her senses. She took Conner with her, giving him no choice but to follow her headlong into the spinning pleasure.

He didn't have the strength to leave her. He lay against her, supporting his weight on his arms to avoid crushing her much smaller frame, but it was beyond his ability to move away from her. His heartbeat rolled like a drum in his ears.

It had been worth waiting for. It was just about worth dying for, he thought, dazed.

He felt Laura shift under him, and he lifted his head from the pillow, looking down at her. In her eyes, he saw the same stunned wonder he felt. Her eyes were all smoky blue, her skin flushed with loving, her mouth soft and swollen from his kisses. He shifted slightly, his chest brushing across her breasts. She caught her breath as crisp curls abraded her swollen nipples. Unconsciously she arched her back, deepening the contact.

It hadn't been enough, he thought almost angrily. He wanted her again, the wanting almost as fierce and hard as it had been the first time. She'd bewitched him, stolen his control, made him forget that it wasn't safe to want the way he wanted her, to need the way he need her. It wasn't safe, not even on this completely physical level.

Conner lowered his head, his tongue finding the pulse that beat too quickly at the base of her throat. Still inside her, he began to harden. Her fingers drifted into the thick dark gold of his hair, pressing against his skull, urging him closer as she opened herself to him, reveling in his possession.

It wouldn't ever be enough, he thought with both anger and despair. And then he stopped thinking and only felt.

Chapter 8

It seemed as if his hunger would never be quenched. If Conner had thought that having her once would be enough, he soon discovered his error. Like a man who'd found an oasis in the desert, he found himself returning to drink from her sweet passion again and again. He woke her twice more in the night, teasing her from sleep with his hands and mouth so that she woke to arousal. Each time, Laura came into his arms with an eagerness that made him ache.

She dropped off to sleep afterward, as quickly and naturally as a child. But there was nothing childlike in the slender body pressed so intimately to his, nor in the fiery response she gave him. She was all woman.

His woman.

Conner had been stroking his hand down Laura's back, but the fierce possessiveness of the phrase made him falter. His woman? He shook his head slightly, as if to shake the thought loose. His wife, yes. But to think of her as his woman implied a deeper commitment than he was willing to admit.

It was bad enough that wanting her had settled like an ache in the pit of his stomach. He wasn't going to add something even more foolish to that. Something like...caring. The physical hunger he could control.

He frowned, thinking of the past two weeks when his control had been something less than satisfactory. All right, if he couldn't control it, at least it could be appeased. She obviously had no objection to being his wife in fact as well as in name. It was his own fault that it had taken so long to discover that. But now that he had, there'd be no more nights spent on the sofa.

Conner nuzzled the soft brown curls that tumbled over the pillows, inhaling the fresh, clean scent of her. His eyelids drifted down as sleep eased over him. His wife, he thought drowsily. His woman. He slept, his arms holding Laura close, his body curled possessively around hers.

Conner was gone when Laura woke, but the scent of him lingered on the pillows. Or perhaps it was on her skin. She wrapped her arms around his pillow and hugged it to her, her mouth curving in a foolish grin. She'd been married for more than two weeks, but this was the first morning she'd felt like a wife. She was disappointed that Conner had left without waking her. It would have been nice to wake the same way she'd gone to sleep—in his arms.

She rolled over and looked at the clock. Six o'clock. By ranch standards, that was practically halfway through the day. She'd yet to master the art of getting up before dawn. But she would. Right now she felt as if she could conquer the world.

Laura swung her legs out of bed, wincing at the stiffness in muscles she'd never had reason to notice. She sat on the side of the bed for a moment, taking stock. She felt ... more. More alive, more sensitive, more a woman. It was as if she'd spent her life half asleep, waiting only for Conner's touch to awaken her. Hadn't she thought something similar the night they'd first made love? Maybe she'd been wiser than she'd thought, recognizing on some deep atavistic level that Conner was ...

Was what? She frowned over the question for a moment and then dismissed it. He was her husband. For now, that was enough.

When Laura entered the kitchen twenty minutes later, she stopped short, surprised to find it occupied. Conner and Gun both sat at the big oak table, half-empty plates in front of them.

"Good morning." Her voice seemed to have gotten caught somewhere in her throat. It came out as little more than a whisper.

"Mornin'." Gun grinned at her and gestured to the stove. "Help yourself. There's batter for more pancakes. Conner ate all the bacon, though." Since there were three strips of crisp meat on Gun's plate, it seemed likely that Conner had had help.

"Considering the amount of food you eat, it's a wonder you don't weigh as much as an ox," Conner commented dryly.

"It takes energy to be as witty and charming as I am," Gun protested, looking hurt.

Conner looked disgusted, but the corner of his mouth turned down as if he was suppressing the urge to grin. Laura chuckled, just as Gun had intended, and moved to the counter to pour herself a cup of coffee. She wondered if she was the only one who'd noticed that Conner hadn't said anything to her.

He'd looked at her when she first came in, those pale green eyes sweeping over her in one long, assessing glance. Laura's knees had weakened as if that look were a touch. But if seeing her made Conner think about how they'd spent the night just past, she couldn't read it in his face. He looked no different than he did on any other morning.

And just as on any other morning, he left the house as soon as he was finished eating. Laura might have thought she'd imagined the night before if it hadn't been for the new awareness inside her, an odd feeling that her body no longer quite belonged to her.

Maybe it was because Gun had been there, she thought, as she poured herself another cup of coffee and loaded the breakfast dishes into the dishwasher. Maybe he hadn't wanted Gun to notice that there'd been a change between the two of them and comment on it.

Laura held on to that thought during the day. Since they were going to be mending fence several miles from the house, the men took sack lunches with them, so she and Mary were on their own for the day. They'd established a routine since Laura's arrival. They had breakfast and then they worked in the garden, though Mary's contribution was generally to find some quiet place where she could sit and dig in the dirt with the spoon Laura had liberated from the kitchen for her.

Most days she conned her stepmother into providing her with water to turn the rich soil into mud pies, which she pressed into the assortment of aluminum tins and flowerpots that Laura gave her.

It was a pleasant way to spend the morning. Laura never tired of working in the garden. It was as if a frustrated plant lover had been lurking inside her just waiting for a chance to escape. Cy and Dottie Williams had visited a few days after her arrival, openly curious to meet Conner's new wife. They'd provided her with a basic gardening book and the advice to keep plenty of blankets handy to guard against the possibility of a late frost.

Tilting her face to the warm sun, it was hard to think of frost, though Gun had confirmed that they could get snow as late as June. Laura smiled, wondering how it was possible that something as foolish as going to bed with a man she'd just met could have resulted in such a wonderful change in her life.

She shifted her eyes to Mary, who was happily splashing mud all over her small coveralls and humming to herself. In two short weeks, she'd learned to love the child as much as if she were her own. Setting her hand against her stomach, she wondered if Conner expected to have more children.

It was something they hadn't discussed. Even in the midst of last night's passion, he hadn't forgotten the need for protection. And he'd been very relieved when she'd been able to tell him that she wasn't pregnant after their first lovemaking. Not that that meant anything. She'd been just as relieved.

But she would like a child of her own, maybe two. Not right away. This marriage was too new, too unsettled for her to be anxious to bring a child into it. But in a few years, perhaps. She narrowed her eyes against the bright sun, pictured herself holding an infant, a little boy with his father's eyes and dark blond hair. Mary would be a doting older sister and, of course, Conner would adore his son.

She frowned, the fantasy stumbling to a halt. Conner showed little outward interest in the child he had. Why would he feel differently about another, especially if he didn't love its mother? But he would love her. Her chin squared with determination and she bent to yank out a small weed that had had the audacity to poke its head aboveground. Love could grow, just like her garden was going to do.

He couldn't have made love to her the way he had last night if he didn't at least *like* her. There'd been more than lust in his touch—she just knew it. He'd only been cool this morning because Gun had been there and he was a very private man, even with his friends.

Her confidence faltered somewhat when Conner's attitude at dinner showed no change from what it had been at breakfast. He didn't show any inclination to want to kiss her or any regret that they didn't have any time alone before she put the meal on the table. He hardly seemed aware of her presence, she thought, feeling hurt and anger gather in her throat.

Once or twice during the meal, their eyes happened to meet, but she could read nothing from this expression. As usual, she thought wrathfully as she tidied the kitchen afterward. And he'd gone back out to the barn with Gun, saying something about checking on a mare that was due to foal soon. Ha! There probably was no mare. He just wanted an excuse to avoid her. It occurred to her that he hadn't seemed to need an excuse before this, but she was too annoyed to listen to such logic, even from herself.

By the time she'd finished getting Mary ready for bed, the annoyance had been replaced by doubt. Maybe last night hadn't been as extraordinary as it had seemed. After all, her experience was severely limited. What had seemed incredible to her might really have been fairly ordinary for a man with some experience. It didn't seem possible that something so breathtaking could be commonplace, but what did she know?

She tucked Mary in, read her a story and then wandered restlessly into the living room. Staring out the window, she saw that there was a light on in the barn, giving credence to Conner's story about the mare. Thrusting out her lower lip, she told herself that only an idiot would feel jealous of a horse.

Turning away from the window, she tried to decide what to do with herself for the remainder of the evening. Television held no appeal, and she finally decided she'd take a book to bed with her. A murder mystery would just about suit her mood.

She chose a novel from the bookshelf in the den and trailed her way to the master bedroom. The bed, where she'd slept alone in reasonable contentment for two weeks, looked suddenly very large and very empty. She doubted Conner would feel the same way and wondered again if she was wrong in thinking that last night had been special.

Well, she'd never know without more experience, and as long as her husband was playing nursemaid to a horse, she wasn't going to have a chance to get any more experience. She dropped the book on the foot of the bed and reached for the buttons on her shirt.

She undressed, tossing her clothes onto the big chair to be dealt with in the morning. Pulling her nightgown out from under the pillow, she turned toward the bathroom. For the first time, she noticed that the door was shut and a narrow edge of light showed beneath it. Before she had a chance to do more than draw in a quick breath, the door was pulled open and her husband stood framed in the doorway.

He'd apparently taken a shower, and he must have shaved because there was no shadow of beard along his jaw. His hair had been toweled until it was damp dry, but he hadn't bothered to comb it, just pushed it back with his hands. He was naked except for the plain white towel that was draped around his hips.

"I thought you were in the barn." It was a mildly foolish thing to say since it was perfectly obvious that he wasn't in the barn, but it was the first thing that popped into her head.

"Sukey decided to wait another day or two." He reached out to switch off the bathroom light.

"Sukey?" Her voice was shaky as he stepped into the bedroom.

"The mare," he reminded her. Halfway across the room, he loosened the knot that held the towel in place. The towel dropped to the floor, but Laura's eyes didn't make it past the heavy length of his arousal.

Breathing suddenly took a conscious effort. Obviously, she could stop worrying about the possibility of him being indifferent to her. Her fingers twisted in the fabric of her nightie. He stopped in front of her. He didn't speak, didn't touch her, didn't do anything but let his pale eyes drift over her.

"You won't be needing this."

She let him take the nightgown. Her heart was beating much too fast. Heat pooled in the pit of her stomach, lapping outward to encompass her entire body. He hadn't even touched her and already she was aching and breathless.

His palms cupped the points of her shoulders. Laura leaned into his touch, and he let his elbows bend until her nipples just brushed the mat of dark gold hair on his chest. She whimpered. An instant later, he had tumbled her back onto the bed and was looming over her, his hips settling into the cradle of her thighs as she opened to him, quivering with need.

"All I've been able to think about all day was how it felt to be inside you," he whispered, his voice guttural. "Heaven on earth."

His mouth caught her cry of welcome as he sheathed himself in her with a heavy thrust, spinning them both toward that heaven.

Laura woke to the sound of the bedroom door closing behind Conner. Her body felt lazy and relaxed but, remembering the morning before, she forced away the urge to fall back against the pillows and simply savor the wonderful feeling of fulfillment. She wanted more from this marriage than incredible sex.

She scrambled into the bathroom and dashed water on her face. After breakfast, she'd take a hot shower and ease away the deliciously achy feeling. She ran a brush through her hair and tugged on jeans and a soft T-shirt. Not exactly regulation seduction attire, but she wasn't trying to seduce him, just to start training him.

When she sauntered into the kitchen, Gun was putting plates on the table and Conner was scrambling what looked like several dozen eggs. She still couldn't get used to the amount of food the two of them put away. Neither of them had an ounce of spare flesh so she assumed the hard work must burn off the calories, but it was going to take some getting used to. Especially the sight of all those eggs at six in the morning.

"Morning." Gun gave her his usual greeting, smiling at her over the rim of his coffee cup. Conner glanced in her direction, his expression enigmatic. He nodded but didn't seem inclined to let himself be distracted from the skillet full of eggs he was stirring.

Well, eggs or nor, she'd made up her mind to show her husband that he couldn't expect to spend the night making love to her and then ignore her the next morning.

"Good morning," she said cheerfully. She smiled at Gun as she walked up to her husband. He was just turning off the heat under the eggs and he turned to look at her, one brow raised in question. He didn't seem much inclined toward conversation in the morning, but that was all right. What she had in mind didn't require words.

Drawing a quick breath and trying to look as if there were nothing extraordinary about the gesture, she set her hand on Conner's chest and raised up on her toes to kiss him. She felt the sudden tension of his muscles beneath her fingers and for one horrifying moment, she thought he might actually jerk away. But perhaps he'd just been shocked by her unexpected action because an instant later, his mouth softened and his hand lifted to cup the back of her head as he deepened the kiss.

She was flushed and breathless when she drew away. Her eyes met his boldly, hoping he'd understood what she was trying to say. She wouldn't be a wife in his bedroom and be invisible outside it. And if she had to repeat the demonstration morning, noon and night, she would. Her mouth curved in a winsome smile as she turned to pour herself a cup of coffee. Come to think of it, that wouldn't be much of a hardship.

"What was she like?" Laura hadn't planned to ask the question, though it had haunted her for weeks. She'd told herself it was none of her business and that looking to the past never did anyone any good. None of the mental lectures helped. She still wanted to know.

"Who?"

They were lying in bed, Laura's head on his shoulder, his fingers idly combing through her hair. Much as she'd enjoyed their lovemaking over the past couple of weeks, she treasured these moments even more. Lying in bed, in her husband's arms, she felt a sense of peace greater than she'd ever known in her life.

The walls were coming down between them. They weren't exactly tumbling. It was more of a brick by brick lowering, but Conner was opening up. He talked about the ranch more, his plans for the future—their future. It was going to take time and patience, but she really believed they could have a good marriage, one based on more than her ability to care for his daughter and their compatibility in bed.

"Rachel. What was she like?"

Conner's hand stilled, and she could almost feel the doors slamming shut.

"She's dead. What does it matter what she was like?"

"She was your wife and Mary's mother. I can't help but wonder what she was like." Laura lifted her head from his shoulder so that she could see his face in the moonlight spilling through the open curtains. His expression was shuttered, his eyes pale as ice and about as revealing.

"Don't wonder," he said flatly. "She's dead. Looking at the past is a waste of time."

He glanced over her shoulder at the clock. "It's late. We'd better get to sleep." And if that wasn't enough to close the topic, the fact that he turned on his side facing away from her was certainly a hint even the most obtuse couldn't have missed.

Stunned, Laura stared at his back. So much for thinking walls were coming down. She sank back onto her pillow and stared up at the darkened ceiling, her breathing slow and careful as she blinked back the tears that threatened. She hadn't been expecting Conner's reaction.

He hadn't talked about his ex-wife. He'd really only mentioned her a couple of times. She'd known that he must have loved her deeply. She'd also thought that he might still be in love Rachel. But over the past couple of weeks, she'd started to think that she might have been wrong. She'd even let herself consider the idea that he didn't talk about Rachel because he thought it might upset her. Obviously, she'd been wrong.

Hurt and anger churned in her stomach. She hadn't asked out of idle curiosity. Rachel was Mary's mother. That alone made her a presence in their lives. Someday, Mary was going to ask about her and she'd need to have answers. Okay, so Mary probably wasn't going to ask tomorrow and she *did* want to know about Rachel for her own sake. But what woman wouldn't be curious about her husband's first wife? There was no reason for Conner to act as if he'd caught her going through his desk.

Maybe he just couldn't bear to talk about her. Maybe he still loves her so much that he can't *talk about her.* The thought slipped in, uninvited, unpalatable and unarguable. Laura blinked back fresh tears. There'd been moments lately when she'd almost forgotten the reason behind her marriage.

Conner's reaction brought the truth crashing back in on her. His motivation for marrying her had been practical, not emotional. If she forgot that, she was going to end up hurt. But things could change. Conner's feelings for her could change. There was no guarantee that he would come to love her, but there wasn't much in life that came with a guarantee. If it was at all possible, she was going to find a way to make her uncommunicative husband fall in love with her.

The decision made, she started considering ways to accomplish her goal. She was in the midst of imagining herself as a world-famous trick rider, riding one of Conner's horses, of course, and thereby bringing

wealth and fame to the Rocking D, when she fell
asleep.

On the other side of the bed, Conner lay awake until nearly dawn, listening to her quiet breathing and
wondering why nothing was turning out the way he'd
expected it would. Wondering why it was that he
hadn't thought of Rachel in days, not until Laura
mentioned her. And wondering how that was possible.

Chapter 9

He always woke before the alarm, reaching out to shut it off before it had a chance to ring and wake Laura. Setting it was a habit more than a necessity. But having lain awake most of the night, this morning he didn't wake until the sharp buzz of the alarm battered against his ears. Feeling like forty miles of bad road, he smacked his hand down on the button to shut it off and swung his legs off the bed.

In a kinder world he would have had a few minutes of peaceful amnesia, but the memory of his abrupt words to Laura the night before was sharp and clear. She was probably angry with him, and he couldn't blame her. He didn't want to talk about Rachel, didn't want to examine the confused tangle of emotions he felt about her. But he shouldn't have cut Laura off so abruptly.

Glancing over his shoulder, all he could see was the back of her head. She lay on her stomach, her head turned away from him, apparently fast asleep. The covers had slipped down, revealing the smooth skin of her shoulders, covered only by the tangled silk of her dark hair.

As always, he felt hunger stir in his gut. Along with it came a sort of puzzled anger. He'd never felt like this before, not even about Rachel. It was as if he were addicted to Laura, to her smell, her touch, the feel of her against him. He'd thought the craving would ease, that once she was in his bed, he'd satiate himself with her and then he'd no longer feel this unending need. Instead, it seemed as if the more he had her, the more he wanted her. Disgusted with himself, he stood up and headed for the bathroom.

"How many Oscars did John Wayne win?" The sleepy voice was muffled by the pillow.

"What?" Startled, Conner stopped and turned to look at the bed.

"How many Oscars did John Wayne win?"

They'd exchanged bits of movie trivia on several occasions since discovering their mutual interest, but it was the last thing he'd been expecting this morning.

"One," he said after a moment. "Everyone knows that."

"It's early." She rolled over and sat up. Conner wasn't sure whether he should be grateful or disappointed that she held the sheet to her chest. She pushed her hair back from her face and frowned at him. "How many times was Henry Fonda nominated for an Oscar?"

"Must have been quite a few." It was his turn to frown while he considered the question. If she was willing to pretend that nothing had happened, he wasn't going to argue with her. "Five."

"Ha! Only twice. *Grapes of Wrath* and *On Golden Pond.*"

"It should have been more."

"Should have doesn't count." She gave him a condescending look down the length of her nose.

"Did anyone ever tell you that you're a poor winner?"

"I simply recognize my natural superiority."

"Maybe we should see just who's superior." He started toward the bed, his eyes holding a wicked gleam.

"Trust a man to resort to brute strength when he's losing intellectually," Laura said, thrusting out one hand as if to hold him off. Her eyes shone with laughter.

"Trust a woman to accuse a man of using brute strength when she knows she's outmatched." Conner put one knee on the bed, his hands wrapping around her shoulders as he tumbled her back against the covers. The remainder of the discussion was strictly nonverbal.

It wasn't as if she were really searching the house, Laura told herself. She was just going through drawers, trying to get a feel for where things were. And if she happened—accidentally—to run across a picture of Conner's first wife, it would be pure coincidence.

By the end of a day spent going through every closet and drawer in the house, such a coincidence had not occurred. She sank down on the sofa, feeling tired and dusty and annoyed with herself. The only room she hadn't looked in was Conner's office. She looked longingly at the door but didn't get up. There were limits, after all. Besides, she didn't really want to know if Conner had a picture of his first wife sitting on his desk. Obviously, if she wanted to know anything about her predecessor, she was going to have to find out by some other means.

"How long have you known Conner?" Laura leaned against the fender of the truck, trying to look casual.

"Ten, maybe twelve years." Gun didn't look up from the engine compartment.

"That's quite a while." Laura picked up one of the spark plugs he'd removed and turned it idly between her fingers. Mary was at the Williamses', where she went two afternoons a week. Cy and Dottie had Cy's sister's children staying with them for the summer and two of them were close to Mary's age. The Williamses insisted that adding one more to the mob created no more work, and Laura thought it was good for Mary to spend time with children her own age. It was worth the long, roundabout drive to get her there.

"It's a fair amount of time," Gun agreed. He removed another plug and set it next to the others.

"You must have known Rachel then," she said, trying to make it sound as if the idea had just occurred to her.

Gun straightened away from the engine and reached for the rag he'd stuck in his back pocket. He studied her and something in his eyes made it clear that she wasn't as good an actress as she'd hoped. Or maybe he was just more perspicacious than she'd wanted to believe.

"I knew Rachel," he said slowly. "Why do you ask?"

"No reason." She lifted one shoulder in a shrug as she set the plug down. "Conner doesn't say much about her."

"Conner doesn't say anything about her," he said bluntly.

She flushed, wishing wholeheartedly that she could say that Conner talked to *her* about his first wife. "No, he doesn't," she admitted with a sigh.

"I don't think he's mentioned her name more than two or three times since she died."

"How did she die?" It was galling to have to ask even that basic question.

"She died when Mary was born."

"Oh!" She'd never considered that as a possibility. She hadn't given it a lot of conscious thought, but she'd had a vague image of some kind of accident, maybe a car wreck. "How terrible!"

"It was rough," he said laconically.

"What was she like?" Laura abandoned any pretense of casual interest. She had the feeling that if she had some understanding of Rachel, she might better understand Conner.

Gun was silent for a moment, his eyes searching her face as if debating whether or not to answer her question. Laura waited, knowing that if he decided not to discuss Rachel with her, there'd be nothing she could say to change his mind.

"She didn't look a thing like you," he said abruptly. "She was a big woman, nearly six foot in her stocking feet. Chestnut hair like Mary's and brown eyes that seemed to laugh most of the time."

He leaned one hip against the fender of the truck and looked into the distance, remembering. Conner had gone to pick up wire for some fencing that needed repair, so there was no question of him interrupting them.

"She wasn't particularly pretty, but you forgot that when she smiled. And she was just about always smiling."

"Where did they meet?" Laura was starting to regret her curiosity. Rachel sounded like a paragon.

"At a rodeo in Arizona. She was raised on a ranch down there. They courted for a few months. She was a few years older than Conner. I guess she was about forty or so when Mary was born. It took him awhile to convince her to marry him."

"I suppose she knew how to ride and everything." Laura gestured with one hand, encompassing the ranch in the "everything."

"She was practically born in the saddle." Gun's expression was sympathetic. "She was one hell of a woman. I won't lie to you and say she wasn't."

"I wouldn't want you to." *Liar. She'd like nothing better than to hear that Rachel had been a dull little dab of a woman, boring and forgettable.* "She sounds nice."

"She was. And Conner loved her. When she died, he burned or gave away everything that had belonged to her. He boxed up a few things and sent them back to her family, but he didn't keep anything of hers around the ranch.''

''Except Mary,'' she whispered, thinking that maybe she finally understood the distance Conner seemed to keep from his daughter.

''Except Mary.'' Gun's eyes confirmed her guess. ''Rachel's folks offered to take her, but he wouldn't allow it.''

So he'd kept Mary with him, but he wouldn't let himself get close to her. Laura felt something close to despair when she thought of how much he must have loved Rachel. She'd really thought there was a chance that he'd come to love her the way she—

She drew in a quick breath as realization washed over her. She loved him. She'd fallen in love with Conner. It wasn't just a matter of making her marriage work or building a future together. She wanted those things, but more than anything she wanted to look into his eyes and see the love she felt reflected there. Aware of Gun's sharp eyes, she turned away, afraid of what he might be able to read in her face. But she hadn't moved quickly enough.

''Conner loved Rachel, but she's dead and he's married to you. That gives you a pretty good advantage.''

''Not if he's still in love with her,'' she said bleakly, beyond trying to pretend that he hadn't read her feelings accurately.

''I'd guess he'll always love her, but that doesn't mean he can't love someone else.'' The kindness in his voice had Laura blinking against the sharp sting of tears.

"He married me to take care of Mary," she admitted. "I'm pretty good at that, but I don't know anything about running a ranch or riding a horse or branding a doggie," she finished bitterly.

Gun's snort of laughter made her turn toward him, shocked that he could be so completely insensitive.

"That's dogie," he said. "One '*g*' not two. Hardly any cowboys brand doggies these days."

Laura smiled reluctantly. "See what I mean. I don't even know the difference between a dog and a cow."

"If Conner had wanted to marry a ranch woman, he could have. He must have had a reason for marrying you."

Guilt that he'd made love to an innocent, she thought, but she didn't say it out loud. This conversation was already more frank than she'd expected.

"Besides, there's nothing to stop you from learning to run a ranch or ride a horse," Gun was saying. "You can even learn to brand a dogie, if you want."

Laura had been spinning toward depression, but his words stopped her short. He was right. She hadn't learned to ride before she could walk and there was nothing she could do to correct that oversight now, but that didn't mean she *couldn't* learn. You didn't have to be born in the saddle to ride. And she could learn about running the ranch. She felt a little less enthusiasm for branding—dogies or anything else. Her impression of the process was vague, but it seemed to involve a lot of dust and noise and hot irons. Still, if that was what it took...

Her eyes grew dreamy. She could get one of those divided skirts and a flat crowned hat and a pair of leather gloves, just like Barbara Stanwyck wore on

"The Big Valley." She had a vision of herself striding down the porch steps, assorted ranch hands jumping to do her bidding. Maybe she'd carry a rifle on her saddle. Never mind that she'd never held a gun in her life. If she could learn to ride, she could learn to shoot. And everyone went armed on the range, didn't they. Protection against . . . against varmints. That was it. Varmints. There'd be no varmints on the Rocking D as long as she had any say about it.

She and Conner would ride the range together, doing whatever one did when one rode the range. Cooking over campfires and things like that. She might be a little vague on details, but she knew exactly how Conner would look at her, the love and admiration in his eyes.

"Laura? You in there?" Gun snapped his fingers in front of her eyes, startling her out of her fantasy. She drew a deep breath, feeling optimism swell inside her, almost drowning out the small, frightened voice that said there was more to gaining Conner's love than learning to ride a horse.

"Can you teach me to ride?" she asked, rushing the words out.

"What?" Gun blinked at her, confused by the quick change of topic.

"You could teach me, couldn't you? It can't be all that difficult. A hundred years ago everybody rode horses, and they can't all have had a talent for it."

"Shouldn't you ask Conner? I'd guess he'd want to be the one to teach you."

"I want to surprise him with it. Please, Gun. Say you'll do it. We could work on it when he's not around."

"I don't know." She bit her lip, giving him a look full of such pleading that he felt his resistance crumble. "I guess I could get you started," he said slowly.

"Thank you! Imagine how surprised he'll be when he finds out."

Gun hoped surprise was all he'd feel. He didn't know the details of his friend's marriage, but he knew that Conner Fox was a possessive man who might not appreciate the idea of his wife and his best friend doing things behind his back, even if it was something innocent. Seeing the love shining in Laura's soft blue eyes, he wondered if Conner had any idea how lucky he was.

Somehow, he doubted it and that was one of the reasons he'd agreed to teach Laura to ride. Conner was bound to find out about the lessons. And maybe when he found out, it would make him take another look at the woman he'd married.

Conner found out even sooner than Gun had anticipated. The next time Mary went to the Williamses' for the afternoon, Conner had an errand in town. He asked if Laura wanted to go with him, thinking she might welcome a chance to get away from the ranch for a little while. Laura made some vague excuses about wanting to try out a new bread recipe. Besides, she really needed to weed the garden before the weeds managed to take over completely. And she'd planned to do some laundry.

Conner was surprised that she'd prefer to stay home doing tasks that could have been done any time, but other than a lifted eyebrow, he didn't argue. He'd been worried that the isolation might bother her. He could hardly complain if it didn't.

In fact, Laura would have loved to go to town with him, not so much to get away from the ranch as for the opportunity to spend time with Conner in a place that couldn't possibly hold any ghosts. But more than that, she wanted to follow through with her plan to become a proper ranch wife. And this was a golden opportunity for her first riding lesson.

Gun didn't share her enthusiasm, but he agreed that this was as good a time as any. As soon as he finished mucking out the stalls, he'd do his best to start her on the road to becoming a horsewoman whose expertise would leave Conner breathless. Laura laughed at his exaggeration, but she flushed a little at the pleasant image.

It was almost an hour before he saddled up one of the horses and led it out into the corral that adjoined the barn. Laura followed him outside and stopped next to him. Now that the moment had come, it struck her that a horse was a very large animal.

"The first thing to remember is not to be afraid of your horse."

"Why?" She'd heard the same thing about strange dogs. "Will it bite?" Noting the size of the mare's teeth, she eased back a half pace.

"They can, but Missy wouldn't dream of biting you. Missy is a lady all the way down to her dainty little hooves."

Missy's hooves looked large and rather sharp to Laura. Not at all what she'd call dainty.

"Here, let her smell you." Gun took her arm and pulled her forward. "Give her a sugar cube."

He demonstrated the flat-palmed presentation. Laura arched her fingers so far back that the tendons ached with the strain. She jumped as the mare lipped the sugar cube from her palm. She was mildly surprised to find that all her fingers seemed to be intact when she lowered her hand.

Watching her, Gun restrained a sigh, mentally scaling back what he'd hoped to get done. She might make a good horsewoman, but first he was going to have to convince her that horses were not carnivorous animals.

They'd progressed to the point where Laura thought she might be willing to actually try sitting on a horse when Conner strode around the corner of the barn. The bulk of building lay between them and the road, blocking the sound of the truck. Conner stopped short, his eyes narrowing at the picture of his best friend bending close to his wife, his voice low and intimate as he talked to her. Laura was looking up at Gun, seeming to hang on his every word.

Conner felt something slam against his breastbone, an emotion that wasn't—couldn't be—jealousy. He couldn't be jealous of Gun. He'd trust him with his life—and had done so on a couple of occasions. *You know how he is with women,* a voice whispered slyly. *And you know how women fall for him.* But not Laura. Laura wouldn't do that, even if Gun would, which he wouldn't.

"Okay, I think I'm ready to give it a try." Laura's words reached him easily.

"Give what a try?"

The startled way they spun to face him would have been funny if he'd been in the mood to see the humor in it.

"Conner!" That was Laura, sounding breathless.

"In the flesh." Conner ducked between the fence rails and walked toward them.

"I thought you were going to be gone all afternoon."

Gun winced, hearing just how damning her words could sound if a person were in the mood to misinterpret them. And the ice in Conner's eyes said that he was perilously close to such a mood.

"Forgot my checkbook," Conner said. "Hope I didn't cause any problems. Coming home unexpectedly."

"No. No, of course not." Laura's breathless laugh rang false. "We were just ... ah ..."

"Laura wanted to learn to ride," Gun said. It was going to come out sooner or later, and he really preferred it to come out before Conner took a swing at him.

Laura threw him a reproachful glance, which he ignored. He recognized the look in Conner's eyes, even if she didn't. And it was too bad that she didn't because she'd probably have been pleased to know that Conner was jealous because of her.

"You're giving her riding lessons?" Conner's voice held surprise, relief and a lingering trace of suspicion.

"That's right."

"I wanted it to be a surprise," Laura muttered, disgruntled that she wasn't going to get to dazzle him with her newly acquired skills. He wasn't likely to be particularly dazzled when she hadn't even made it into the saddle yet. And the jeans and loafers she wore were a far cry from the dashing split skirt she'd imagined.

Conner's eyes cut from Gun to Laura and then back to his friend. "If my wife wants to learn to ride, I'll teach her." The words were blatantly possessive, a subtle challenge from one male animal to another.

"Fine by me," Gun said. "I told Laura you'd be a better teacher."

"Are you sure you wouldn't mind?" Laura asked, looking up at her husband. She'd completely missed the byplay between the two men, as well as the possessiveness in Conner's stance. She was just pleasantly surprised that Conner would want to teach her to ride.

"I don't mind." In fact, it annoyed him that he hadn't thought of it before. Of course, she needed to know how to ride. Isolated as the ranch was, there might come a time when she'd *need* to know how.

He moved over to the horse, checking the saddle automatically. It wasn't a matter of doubting Gun's ability to saddle a horse, it was simply the normal precaution of someone who spent a good portion of his life in the saddle and had learned never to take anything for granted.

Gun's brows rose slightly when Conner lengthened the stirrups, but he didn't comment. Nor did he comment when Conner swung up into the saddle and then reached his hand down to Laura. Gun doubted she'd learn a whole hell of a lot about riding that way, but then he didn't think Conner was as interested in her learning to ride at the moment as he was in making sure that there was no doubt about just whose wife she was.

"I don't think you two need any help from me," he said. "I'll just go do some ... things in the barn."

"Thank you, Gun." Laura smiled over her shoulder at him.

"You're welcome." He noticed that Conner didn't seem to think it was necessary to add his thanks to Laura's. Suppressing a grin, he turned and went into the barn.

Laura hardly noticed his departure. She was too busy following Conner's instructions. She set her foot in the stirrup and then gave a startled gasp as he pulled her up into the saddle in front of him. She clutched automatically at the saddle horn.

"Relax," he told her, his breath brushing against her hair.

"It's a lot higher than I'd expected," she said, staring at the ground.

"I'm not going to let you fall." He slid his boot into the stirrup and nudged the mare into a walk.

Laura gasped and tightened her grip on the saddle horn, her knuckles turning white with the force she was exerting. Conner said nothing. He simply walked the mare around the corral, letting her get the feel of the animal's motion. After a minute, she relaxed a little, easing deeper in the saddle. He nearly groaned as her bottom settled snugly against the fly of his jeans.

Telling himself to keep his thoughts above his belt buckle, Conner guided the mare to the gate. When he leaned down to open it, Laura clutched at the saddle horn again, but once they were through, she relaxed quickly. He hadn't fooled himself any more than Gun about his reasons for taking Laura up in front of him. He'd wanted—needed—to stake a claim.

Laura was unaware of his motives and didn't have enough experience to know that his teaching methods were not exactly standard. What she did know was that it felt wonderful to be held so close against him. She leaned farther back, feeling the broad muscles of his chest supporting her, the strength of his arms on either side of her.

She only half listened to what he was saying, something about learning to move with the horse, feeling the rhythm of the animal's movement and going with it, not against it. She couldn't have said just what the horse was doing, but she could feel every move Conner made.

"Now you try guiding her." She took the reins from him, wondering if he'd told her what to do with them. The mare continued to plod up the road, the path she'd been on since leaving the ranch yard. Laura held one rein in each hand, stared between Missy's pointed ears and wondered what she was supposed to do next.

"Remember, she'll go in the direction you tug. You don't have to pull hard. She's got a soft mouth."

"Is that good?"

"That's good." Conner's chuckle sounded next to her ear. "It means it doesn't take much pressure for her to understand what you want. Just a little tug." He put his hand over hers and demonstrated, and Laura was shocked when Missy obediently turned to the right, ambling off the dirt road and into the pasture.

"She turned!" She twisted in the saddle to smile at him. The movement pressed the side of her breast firmly against Conner's arm. It also snuggled her more solidly into the cradle of his thighs. She was abruptly aware of his arousal pressed against her bottom. And if she hadn't been, Conner's hand shifting almost convulsively to cover her breast would certainly have given her a strong clue.

As always, all it took was a touch and she melted. Her head fell back against his shoulder, the movement thrusting her breast more firmly into his hold. His touch burned even through the fabric of her shirt. His head lowered, and she gasped as she felt his teeth score the taut arch of her neck.

If he chose to slide off the horse and make love to her in the middle of the pasture in broad daylight, Laura wasn't sure she could lift a finger to protest. Heat was already pooling in her stomach, lapping out to warm her entire body. But if she was on the verge of forgetting where they were, Conner was not quite so far-gone.

"Damn." He straightened in the saddle and took the reins from her lax fingers. Clicking his tongue at the mare, he turned her back toward the ranch. He nudged her into a fast walk.

Neither of them spoke. Laura didn't think she could have found her voice if her life had depended on it. Conner's body was rigid with tension as they rode into the yard. He stopped Missy beside the corral. Laura assumed he was going to help her to dismount, but for an instant his hand flattened against her stomach, his fingers splaying over her, heat penetrating her cotton shirt as he held her. And then he'd taken her arm and she was sliding off the horse to stand on the hard-packed dirt with no clear idea of how she'd come to be there.

Conner turned the horse toward the gate, and Laura saw him lean down to open it. Turning, she made her way toward the house. Her knees were more than a little iffy about supporting her but she made it, climbing up the porch steps and letting herself into the house. Once inside, she wasn't sure what to do with herself.

She stared around the living room as if it were an alien landscape. There'd been no indication that Conner planned to follow her up to the house. Except to have lunch, he rarely set foot in the house during the day. Probably he was going to go into town. After all, that's where he would have been if he hadn't forgotten his checkbook.

Feeling achy and restless, she went into the kitchen. She had the vague idea that an ice-cold drink might help cool the heat that made her feel almost feverish. She'd just taken out a pitcher of iced tea when she heard the front door open and then close. There was something definitive in that click.

Laura's fingers knotted around the pitcher's handle as she heard Conner's footsteps going down the hall. There was a moment's silence, and she wondered if he'd expected her to be in the bedroom. And then he was returning. Aware of the fine tremor in her fingers, she set the pitcher on the counter, moving very carefully to avoid dropping it.

And then Conner was stepping into the kitchen. Their eyes met, and Laura felt his hunger wash over her, arousing her as surely as his touch. He stopped in front of her, looking down at her with that half-angry expression that she never quite understood. Then his hand came up, his fingers burrowing into her hair, snapping the rubber band that held it back. His mouth came down on hers, hot and hard. With a soft whimper, Laura opened to him, her body like a flame in his arms.

They didn't make it to the bedroom. They got as far as the living room where Conner pressed her down onto the thick sheepskin rug in front of the empty fireplace. Buttons popped and seams tore as they struggled to undress each other.

He entered her with one powerful thrust. She cried out with pleasure as her body adjusted to hold him, welcome him. This was not a time for soft caresses and lingering kisses. It was quick and hot and hard. The fulfillment, when it came, was as powerful as the hunger that drove them toward it. Laura's nails scored his back, her body arching as if to throw him from her even as her legs drew him deeper. Conner arched over her, the skin stretched taut over his cheekbones as the pulse of his climax rushed over him.

When he collapsed against her, Laura welcomed his heavy weight. In moments like this, she knew he was hers completely. With a deep womanly instinct, she knew there were no ghosts between them in this.

It was several minutes before she found the breath to speak. She longed to be able to tell him she loved him. Now that she knew how she felt, it was difficult to hold the words back. But it was too soon. He wasn't ready to hear that from her.

"If I'd known that riding lessons were this much fun, I'd have suggested them sooner." Her voice was breathless but rich with humor.

Conner laughed against her throat before gathering his strength to roll away from her. "Too many riding lessons like that could just about kill me."

"But what a way to go."

He laughed again and slid his arm under her, drawing her against his side. It was always the same. The incredible intensity of their lovemaking followed by a rich contentment he'd never known. He couldn't shake the feeling that he had no business feeling the way he did, but the niggling doubts couldn't impinge on his mood. He felt deeply, completely contented. Laura's next words made the contentment fade somewhat.

"You should teach Mary to ride." Her tone was idle, as was the movement of her fingers against his chest. "Maybe we could take lessons together. It might help her to see that I'm learning, too."

Conner shifted uneasily. "Gun can teach her to ride," he muttered.

"Mary. Her name is Mary." She rolled onto her stomach and propped herself on her elbows so that she could look down at him. "Do you know you never use her name?"

"What are you talking about?" The contentment was a fast fading memory. Conner eyed her warily. "Of course I use her name."

"No, you don't." She frowned at him but it was a look of puzzlement rather than annoyance. "You call her 'the child' or 'her' but you never call her 'Mary.'"

"That's ridiculous. Mary. See, I used her name." He almost winced at the defensive sound of his own voice.

"Good. You can practice using it while you're teaching her to ride."

"Gun's perfectly capable of teaching her to ride." He sat up, reaching for the clothes he'd discarded so hastily only a few minutes before.

"I'm sure Gun would be a terrific teacher," Laura agreed, her tone the essence of sweet reason. "But you're her father, and I think you should be the one to teach her."

"I run a ranch, not a riding academy," he muttered. He struggled to untangle his shirt from her jeans.

"If you don't have time to teach us both, then you can teach Mary while Gun teaches me."

"No!" The word was sharper than he'd intended. He saw Laura's brows climb. "I'll teach you."

"But if Gun is good enough to teach Mary, then I'm sure he's more than good enough to teach me."

"I'll teach you," he said in a tone that brooked no argument. It wasn't that he didn't trust Gun. It was just that if he ever saw him with his hands on Laura, he doubted he'd be able to control the urge to knock the man into the middle of next month. He tugged angrily at the tangled clothes. Her shirt seemed to have twined itself around his jeans. The same way she'd twined herself around his life. He suddenly felt as if he were suffocating.

"But you're Mary's father—"

"I'll teach the child too," he snapped. He caught her look and amended his statement. "*Mary*. I'll teach Mary to ride, too."

"Good." Laura gave him a sweet smile. Seeing his struggles, she reached out and took the garments from

him, deftly separating them and then handing him his
jeans.

Conner stared at her for a moment, uncertain as to
how he'd come to agree to do something he'd had no
intention of doing. He didn't want to teach the child
to ride. *The child.* Did he really avoid using her name?
The habit must be so ingrained that he wasn't even
aware of it.

He shook his head, dismissing the question. He
didn't have time to psychoanalyze himself. He had a
ranch to run and he couldn't run it from here. Though
it was tempting to try, he thought, casting a regretful
look at Laura's nude body.

Conner stood up and thrust one leg into the denim
and then almost overbalanced and fell flat on his face
with her next words.

"Mary looks so much like you, you know." She was
sliding her arms into the sleeves of her madras shirt
and didn't see the stunned look he gave her.

Like him? Every time he looked at her, he saw her
mother. Her hair was the same color as Rachel's and
sometimes when she smiled, it was like looking at his
dead wife in miniature. Look like him? Not that he'd
ever noticed.

Shaking his head, he decided that it must be a female thing, like their ability to look at a red-faced,
squash-nosed infant and announce with certainty that
she had Great-Aunt Edna's eyebrows and Uncle Je-
hosephat's chin.

The child—Mary—looked no more like him than
she looked like Gun.

Chapter 10

"Oh, drat. I forgot the flour." Laura frowned at the grocery sacks that nearly filled the bed of the truck.

"Considering all these sacks, it doesn't seem possible that you left anything in the store," Conner said. He lifted the last bag from the cart and set it with the others before slamming the tailgate shut.

"Well, I left the flour and I've got to get some." She looked down at Mary who was leaning tiredly against her leg. It had been her idea to bring the little girl into town with them, since it seemed a terrific opportunity to get Conner and his daughter together.

When Conner had said that he refused to teach anyone wearing loafers to ride, a trip into town had become essential. And since she no longer needed to take advantage of his occasional absences to sneak in a riding lesson, Laura had been anxious to see what the nearest town of any size was like.

It was much like any other town, crowded, smelling of car exhaust and noisy. Funny, she'd never noticed just how noisy cities were until she'd spent a few weeks away from them. Not that this was exactly a metropolis, but it was large enough to provide an effective advertisement for the pleasure of country living.

She might have gone along with Conner's suggestion that they leave Mary off at the Williamses' if she'd realized just how long the day was going to be for a three-year-old. First they'd stopped at the bank, where Conner had opened a checking account in her name. Laura hadn't given much thought to money and she was touched that he obviously had.

From there, they'd gone to purchase the boots he said she had to have if she wanted to learn to ride. They were black and very plain, but she thought the pointed toes and low heels made her look positively Western. When she said as much, Conner grinned at her and plopped a beige cowboy hat on her head and the look was complete. While he paid for the purchases, she admired her reflection in the mirror. It wasn't exactly Barbara Stanwyck, but it would do. And anyone who looked as authentic as she did should be a natural for riding.

They'd stopped for lunch, devouring tacos and soda. It was after the meal that Mary had started to run out of energy, and Laura was annoyed with herself for not having given more thought to the fact that she usually went down for a nap after lunch. Obviously it was going to take a while for her to learn to think like a mother at all times.

Conner left them off at the supermarket while he ran a couple of his own errands. Mary, usually the most agreeable of children, showed a less than sunny side. Cranky and tired, she fussed her way through the store until Laura finally succumbed to one of the oldest temptations of motherhood and bribed her with an ice-cream bar. It kept the child quiet long enough for Laura to get to the checkout counter.

Conner was waiting for them when they walked out of the store, and she thought she'd never seen a more beautiful sight than the boxy lines of the pickup. She was as tired and felt nearly as cranky as the little girl clinging to the hem of her skirt.

Conner had rarely seen a more bedraggled pair. There was chocolate ice cream smeared all over Mary's face and decorating her pale blue coveralls. Small, hand-shaped stains on the hem of Laura's skirt showed where Mary had grabbed and clung. All Laura wanted was to go home, have a hot shower and then sit and stare at the walls until her jangling nerves quieted. And she might have been able to do just that if she hadn't forgotten the stupid flour.

She looked from her list to Mary. There was no way she was taking her back into the store.

"You keep an eye on her. I'll only be a minute."

"But I—" She wasn't listening. She'd bent over to talk to Mary.

"You be a good girl for Daddy, okay?"

"'kay." Mary's agreement came on a tired sigh, and Laura brushed a quick kiss across her ice-cream-smeared cheek.

"I'll only be a minute," she said again. The promise seemed equally directed toward both Conner and the little girl.

Conner opened his mouth to suggest that *he* should be the one to go get the missing flour, but she had already thrust Mary's sticky hand into his and was hurrying back toward the store. He dragged his eyes from her retreating back to look down at his daughter. She looked back up at him solemnly.

"You're dirty," he said after a moment.

"Ice meem," she informed him. She rubbed her hand over her face as if to wash away the evidence, but all she succeeded in doing was smearing it a little more. It was Conner's guess that nothing short of steel wool would get the chocolate stains off her face.

"Good," she added, as if that excused the mess, which he supposed it did.

That topic of conversation exhausted, they stared at each other in silence. Conner racked his brain, wondering what one said to a three-year-old. He doubted she'd be interested in the fact that beef prices had dropped again. Nor was she likely to care that the Broncos might have a better team this next season than they had in the last.

He glanced around the parking lot, hoping for inspiration, but nothing occurred to him. They could sit in the truck and wait for Laura, but the sun beating down on the cab made it hot and stuffy.

Mary seemed to feel none of the indecision that gripped her father. Taking hold of his pant leg and depositing a series of smudgy fingerprints in the process, she tugged to get his attention. When she saw that she had it, she pointed to the front of the store.

"Ride." It was clearly a demand.

"Ride?" It took him a moment to realize what she must be pointing to. Set to one side of the entrance was a plastic pony ride. A boy of about six was rocking happily on its back while his mother stood and watched. "You want to ride the pony?"

"Hosey," she confirmed. Having no doubts that he'd agree, probably sensing that he'd agree to almost anything at the moment, Mary lifted her arms for him to pick her up.

"Okay." Conner settled her against his hip, balancing her easily with one arm around her back. Though he'd carried her the same way many times before, it struck him suddenly how very small she was, how dependent she was on the adults in her life to care for her.

When the little boy got off, Conner settled Mary astride the plastic horse, making sure that she had a good grip on the bar that substituted for reins before he put a quarter in the slot. Immediately the horse began to move. Mary's eyes widened and her tiny fingers clutched the steel bar even tighter. She seemed to be debating whether or not she liked the treat she'd requested, her expression flickering uncertainly between a smile and a frown. The debate was settled when she looked at her father, her eyes sparkling, her small face creased in a wide grin.

Conner was surprised to find himself grinning back, enjoying her pleasure. It struck him as ironic that she lived on a ranch with an ample supply of real horses and yet her first ride was on a plastic horse in front of a supermarket. Laura was right—Mary should start learning to ride. She was old enough to begin on a gentle horse. With him there to keep an eye on her, she'd be all right.

Looking at her, he was struck by the odd feeling that he was seeing her for the first time, seeing her as something more than a reminder of all he'd lost. He suddenly realized that he'd never really looked beyond the chestnut shade of her hair, the same warm color as her mother's. But other than that, there was little about her that reminded him of Rachel. Neither did he see the resemblance to him that Laura claimed to have noticed. She looked like...Mary. She was her own small person, completely separate from the two people who'd given her life.

He didn't see Laura come out of the store and stop when she saw him with Mary. She watched the two of them, saw the look of reluctant wonder on Conner's face and felt hope swell inside her. Maybe, just maybe, this miserable trip would accomplish more than she'd hoped. If Conner could just *see* Mary, really see her as something other than a reminder of the wife he'd lost, she couldn't believe he'd be able to continue to hold her at a distance.

From the way he was looking at the little girl, she dared to hope that the first step had been taken. Given time, the three of them could become a real family. She didn't think Rachel would begrudge her that dream.

The riding lessons went surprisingly well. Laura didn't know whether looking the part actually made it easier to learn, but it certainly didn't hurt. Wearing the new boots and hat made the horses seem less intimidating somehow, as if they'd be less inclined to decide to divest themselves of someone with the proper accoutrements.

As he'd promised, Conner also started teaching Mary to ride. At first, he only took her up in front of him, letting her get the feel of the horse while being held safely in his arms. After a few sessions like that, he put her into the saddle alone, choosing an older horse with a gentle temperament. Laura held her breath when she saw the little girl perched on top of the big horse. She had to bite her tongue to hold back the urge to say that she'd changed her mind—that Mary was too young to learn to ride.

Conner stayed right beside the horse, one hand on the animal's neck, the other resting on the cantle, ready to snatch the child from the saddle if anything went wrong. But Mary took to riding like a born horsewoman, showing no fear at all. And Conner's pride at her courage might have been reluctant, but it was also unmistakable.

Watching the two of them, Laura felt a swell of emotion that could not have been stronger if Mary had been a child of her own body. Nothing was going to happen overnight, but with each day that passed, she sensed an easing in Conner. It was as if he'd been holding himself tightly checked for a long time and was slowly learning how to let go of the feelings and emotions he'd been denying for the past three years.

It seemed as though when Rachel died, he'd made a decision—conscious or not—that he'd never let anyone matter that much to him again. And that had included his daughter. But the walls he'd built were starting to show cracks, and Laura was determined to keep chipping away at them until the walls disappeared completely.

As spring eased into summer, Laura knew that she'd never been happier in her life. It was hard to believe that she'd taken such a crazy chance in marrying a man she barely knew and that the gamble would pay off so handsomely. She had a home, a wonderful daughter—because she already thought of Mary as her own—and a husband she loved more than she'd have thought possible.

There were still problems. Conner never spoke of Rachel, and sometimes she felt a cold fear that he'd never allow another woman into his heart, that the biggest part of him would always lie with Rachel, buried away, never to live again. But Rachel was gone, and from what Gun had said about her, Laura couldn't believe that she'd have wanted Conner to grieve forever. Laura didn't begrudge her the past she'd shared with Conner, she only wanted a chance at a future with him.

Her life in L.A. seemed as if it had belonged to someone else entirely, and in a way it had. It had been Laura Halloran who'd worked as a cocktail waitress and wondered if her life was going to slide by without her ever having a chance to live it. Laura *Fox* had a husband, a child and a future.

She found the last of her bitterness toward her mother fading away, leaving behind a profound pity. Billie had missed so much. She'd never been able to see beyond the moment, never had the courage to take a chance on building something that would last more than a few nights. She hadn't even been able to let herself accept the love Laura would have been more than willing to give her. She'd died a lonely, bitter woman, old before her time.

Laura would never know for sure whether or not she'd have ended up on the same destructive path her mother had taken. She wanted to think that she was stronger than that. But it was no longer a concern. No matter what would happen with her marriage, she'd learned that she controlled her own fate. And that taking risks was what made life worth living. Now if only she could convince Conner to take a risk on loving her.

After a month of riding lessons, she felt confident enough to take Missy out on her own. She and the mare had become friends, or so Laura liked to think. In her more rational moments, she suspected that Missy's friendship was predicated largely on Laura's unending supply of sugar cubes. However, she was willing to take equine friendship where she found it and not examine motives too closely.

Gun had taken the day off and gone into town. He took Mary with him when he left in the morning, saving Laura from making the trip to the Williamses' so that Mary could play with The Horde, as Cy and Dottie referred to the conglomeration of children— theirs and their relatives' who were spending the summer with them. Conner had ridden out even before Gun left, getting an early start on the day's work of repairing fences, an endless job on any ranch. Since Conner had taken his lunch with him, Laura knew she'd have the day to herself.

For the first few hours, she savored the quiet. Much as she loved Mary, she couldn't deny that it was nice to have a few hours when she didn't have to worry about keeping her entertained or fed or making sure that she wasn't doing something that might prove dangerous.

Laura puttered around the house. With each passing day, it seemed to belong more and more to her and less and less to the woman who'd preceded her there.

Once the house was tidy, Laura went outside to spend some time in the garden. Cy had provided her with two rosebushes for the flower beds she was putting in on either side of the front step. When she'd mentioned the idea to him, Conner had commented that his mother had had flower beds there. After her death, there'd been no one who shared her interest in taking care of them and they'd gradually succumbed to time and neglect.

Which meant Rachel hadn't been a gardener. Laura took some satisfaction from the thought. It was nice to know there were a few areas where she didn't have to compete with a memory.

By midafternoon, she was starting to tire of her own company. Mary could be exhausting, but she was never boring. And with Conner and Gun both gone, as well, the ranch seemed very empty. Wandering out to the barn, she fed Missy a sugar cube.

"You look as lonely as I feel," she said, scratching the mare's forehead. Missy nudged Laura's shoulder with her nose. She was probably looking for more treats, but Laura chose to take it as a suggestion. "You want to blow this joint?"

Missy's snort sounded like agreement, and an instant later Laura was opening the stall door and leading her out. Since Conner had insisted that learning to saddle a horse was part of learning to ride one, it wasn't long before she was leading the mare to the stump that Gun had placed next to the barn for her when it became obvious that she couldn't get into the saddle without a boost.

Settling into the saddle, Laura grinned, feeling her vague melancholia fall away as she nudged the mare into a walk. A few weeks ago she had hardly known which end of a horse was which. Now she was practically an expert.

Expert or no, she kept the pace to a walk as she pointed the mare's nose toward the mountains that loomed behind the ranch. It was a beautiful early summer day. The sky was an endless blue bowl, unmarked by a single cloud. She was young, healthy and in love with the man she'd married. She even felt remarkably optimistic about him returning that love in time. It would have been difficult to imagine a more perfect day.

It was late afternoon when Conner drove back into the ranch yard. He was hot and sweaty. He hoped that the unseasonably warm weather wasn't an indication of what the rest of the summer was going to be like. If it was, there might be problems with the water supply. He'd probably be okay, even if there was a fullfledged drought. He didn't run a large herd of cattle and since they weren't the ranch's main source of income, he could cut even that back to almost nothing.

Besides, according to what his father had told him, there'd never been a time when the Rocking D ran out of water. His grandfather had carefully selected the ranch site and there'd always been enough water. But

there was a first time for everything. Besides, he knew
a lot of other ranchers who weren't so well situated.
Even one season's worth of drought would be enough
to put some of them under.

He stepped down out of the truck and dust puffed
up from the dirt. There was no sense in worrying
about something that probably wasn't going to happen, but he knew he wouldn't be the only one watching the sky and wondering. Water was an ever-present
concern in the West, dominating everything from
politics to landscaping.

He took off his hat as he walked up to the house.
Lifting one arm, he blotted the sweat off his forehead
onto his shirtsleeve. He wanted a cool shower and a
cold beer, not particularly in that order.

Gun's car was gone, which meant he must still be in
town, unless he'd just decided to keep on driving.
With Gun that was always a possibility. He'd been
moving since Conner first met him, rarely staying in
any one place more than a few months, sometimes
leaving after a couple of weeks.

They'd gotten drunk together one night quite a few
years ago and Conner had asked him why he didn't
settle down, get himself a place of his own and build
toward the future. There was nothing Gun didn't
know about ranching. The bleakness in Gun's eyes
had penetrated even the whiskey-induced haze in
Conner's brain.

"If I stay in one place too long, I might catch up
with myself," Gun had told him. Drunk as he was,
Conner had known exactly what he meant. The sad
part was that whatever Gun was running from, he
carried it inside himself. And you could never run fast

enough to escape something like that. If whatever it was that haunted him was creeping up on him again, Gun might take off, but he usually said goodbye, so chances were, he just hadn't gotten back from town yet.

Conner pushed open the front door and stepped inside, letting the cool welcome of the living room enfold him. It occurred to him suddenly that it had been a long time since he'd thought of the house in terms of welcome. After Rachel died, it had become nothing more than a shelter, a place to eat and sleep, holding little more value to him than if it were a shack in the wilderness.

Since Laura had been here, it had become a home again. The change had been slow. Or maybe he'd simply been slow to notice it. He paused in the archway that led into the living room, looking at the room as if seeing it for the first time. The drapes were drawn open and the room was filled with sunlight. There were magazines scattered on the coffee table and a stack of Mary's toys in one corner. One of his shirts was draped over the arm of the sofa, a needle and thread still in the patch she was sewing over a three-corner tear near the hem. The room looked lived in. It looked loved.

A memory niggled at the back of his mind of the last time he'd seen the room like this, felt the house welcome him when he opened the door. Fifteen years ago, when his mother was alive, he thought slowly. Like Rachel, she'd been ranch born and bred and she could ride like a Comanche and turn her hand to almost any outdoor task that presented itself. But she'd preferred the traditional feminine role, making a home for her family, baking and tending the garden.

When she was alive, he'd felt this same sense of welcome, a feeling of having come home that went deeper than simply stepping in out of the weather. He shook his head and turned away from the gently cluttered room. He was starting to get fanciful in his old age.

It didn't take long to realize that the house, for all its welcome, was empty. Laura must have gone to pick up Mary, he thought. He took his beer along to the bathroom with him. There were still chores to be done, but he had dirt embedded in every pore. He could even feel grit between his teeth. He'd shower again later, if necessary.

Laura still wasn't back when he left the house half an hour later, wearing clean clothes, his hair still damp. Between the cold beer and the shower, he was feeling almost human. The sun was starting to sink behind the mountains and their long shadows spilled across the ranch yard.

Conner's hand was on the barn door latch when it occurred to him that he'd parked the truck next to Laura's car. He'd bought the vehicle from Cy Williams a couple of weeks before. It wasn't new, but it was solid and would provide Laura with reliable transportation so that she didn't have to depend on him or Gun to take her anywhere she needed to go.

And it had been parked in its usual spot beside the barn. So if she hadn't taken the car to go pick up Mary, where was she? It wasn't that she had to be in sight at all times, but it seemed odd that she hadn't greeted him the way she usually did. He turned away from the barn and started toward the back of the house, thinking that maybe she was working in the garden. But he'd gone only a few steps when he heard the sound of Gun's car coming up the road.

Conner stopped and turned to watch the red Corvette roar over the dirt road, kicking up a cloud of dust that lingered behind it in the still air. It was a ridiculous car for a cowboy, as Conner had pointed out on more than one occasion. It was an even more ridiculous car for a man as big as Gun. He just about wore it rather than rode in it.

But Conner's thoughts weren't on the car's suitability or lack thereof. Maybe Gun had come back early and then for some reason, he and Laura had taken his car over to the Williamses'. But when the car stopped, Conner could see that Laura wasn't in it. Gun got out and went around to open the passenger door. He leaned in to unbuckle Mary's seat belt. She scrambled out of the car and trotted up to Conner.

"Pictures." She thrust a sheaf of multicolored paper up at him, and he smiled as he took it from her.

Gun wondered if Conner even realized how much things had changed around here since Laura's arrival. A couple of months ago, it wouldn't have occurred to Mary to show her artistic efforts to her father, any more than it would have occurred to Conner to leaf through them. They weren't exactly the closest father and daughter he'd ever seen, but they were making progress.

"'Aura want to look," Mary informed him as she took the drawings back from him.

"Laura's not here," Conner told her. He shifted his attention to Gun. "I thought maybe she'd gone with you."

"Nope. I took Mary over to Cy and Dottie's this morning and I told her I'd pick her up when I came back this afternoon. She's not here?" It was a superfluous question. Obviously, Laura wasn't there or Conner wouldn't have thought she was with him.

"I got back a little less than an hour ago and I haven't seen her. Her car's still here."

"Maybe she went for a walk."

"Maybe." The thought was not particularly reassuring. A lot of things could happen on a walk, especially to someone more accustomed to concrete sidewalks than sagebrush. Rattlesnakes occasionally showed up in the ranch yard. They were considerably more common beyond it. And there was always the possibility of a missed step resulting in a sprained ankle or a broken leg.

"Maybe she's out back, working in the garden," Gun suggested, reading Conner's thoughts.

"She might not have heard the truck, but no one could miss hearing the engine in that thing." He nodded to the Corvette. "It'd damn near wake the dead."

"Power comes with a price," Gun said, automatically continuing an old argument.

"Yeah, well, she'd have heard it if she were anywhere in the county."

"Just because she didn't, doesn't mean there's anything wrong."

"'Aura sick?" Mary had apparently picked up on their worry. She curled her fingers around the side of Conner's jeans and looked up at him. "'Aura sick?"

"No. She's not sick. She's not here right now, but she's fine. She'll be home in a little while."

But he felt less sure of that a few minutes later when he checked the barn and found Laura's favorite mount missing.

"She's a pretty fair rider," Gun said when Conner told him what he'd found.

"She's not good enough to go wandering around on her own." Conner braced his hands on his hips and frowned down at Mary, who was hunkered down watching a black beetle make its way across the dusty yard. "Besides, it's getting late. Why isn't she back yet?"

"Probably went farther than she thought. You know how deceptive that can be. I bet she'll ride in any minute now."

As if in response to his words, Missy ambled into the yard moments later. But there was nothing particularly reassuring about her arrival. The saddle was empty and she held her head to the side, walking with a slightly mincing step as she tried to avoid stepping on the reins that trailed along the ground.

Conner felt as if he'd been kicked in the stomach. In an instant, a dozen possibilities flashed through his mind. All of them had one common image: Laura thrown from the saddle to lie broken and bleeding on the ground.

The mare shied as he approached her, perhaps sensing the tension in him. His eyes went over her, checking for injury, checking for any clue as to what might have happened to her rider.

"Even if she was thrown, it doesn't mean she was hurt." Gun had come up behind him and had given the mare the same visual once-over. "Could be she got off on her own and the mare just wandered off."

"Yeah." He knew Gun was right. That was the simplest explanation. There was no reason to assume the worst. He took the mare's reins and led her toward the barn. "Saddle the gray for me, would you?"

"I'll go with you."

"One of us has to stay with Mary," Conner said, nodding to where she still hunkered in the dirt.

"Of course. Besides, you'll probably find her halfway home by now. And I bet those new boots of hers hurt like the devil."

"Probably." Conner's smile was strained.

Twenty minutes later, he was heading out of the yard, going in the direction the mare had come from. He had a sleeping bag tied behind the saddle, a canteen and some trail rations thrown in his saddlebag. Considering the lateness of the hour, there was a good chance that once he found Laura, it would be too late to try and start back.

Gun, with Mary settled comfortably on his hip, watched Conner leave. Remembering the look on his friend's face when the mare had come back alone, he wondered if Conner had any idea just how much his wife meant to him. Whatever their reasons for marrying in the first place, they could make it a real love match, if only Conner would let it happen.

At that moment, Conner's thoughts about his missing wife were not exactly filled with affection. They wavered between a hope that she was safe and unhurt and the determination that, if she was all right, he was going to throttle her when he found her.

She was so small and she didn't have the faintest idea of how to take care of herself. She was too trusting, for one thing. Look at the way she'd trusted him. Not only had she slept with him but she'd married him, for God's sake. And if she hadn't been able to protect herself in the city, she sure as hell didn't know how to take care of herself in the wilderness. Would she even have the sense to stay in one place and wait to be found or was she wandering around getting herself lost?

Assuming she wasn't so badly hurt that she couldn't walk at all, of course.

His thinking veered from one image to the next—finding her alive and well and shaking her until her teeth rattled, then finding her unconscious, perhaps badly injured.

And if he didn't find her soon, it was going to be too dark to look.

The last of the light was just fading when he found her. She was sitting on a rock, not far off the main trail. She had her left ankle propped on her right knee, the boot off, her fingers massaging the sole of her foot. Relief swelled in his throat, choking off anything he might have said, but she must have heard the gray's approach because she looked up, her smile gleaming in the twilight.

"Conner! Boy, am I glad to see you." She started to slide off the rock, remembered her missing boot and picked it up, grimacing as she slid her aching foot into it. "These boots aren't made for walking," she commented.

Conner did not smile. He slid the rifle out of its sheath and, pointing it toward the sky, fired off two shots. Laura jumped as the sound echoed off the mountains.

"What was that for?"

"To let Gun know you're alive." They were the first words he'd spoken and there was a quality in his voice that made her peer up at him a little uneasily.

"Of course I'm alive. Why shouldn't I be?"

"No reason. Don't they claim that God watches out for fools and children? Give me your hand."

She obeyed automatically, turning his words over in her mind. With easy strength, Conner swung her up behind him. Laura settled herself as comfortably as she could and put her arms around his waist.

"I didn't mean to worry you," she ventured.

"We're going to have to camp tonight," he said, ignoring her apology. "I don't want to risk the horse putting his foot in a rabbit hole in the dark."

Laura didn't argue. She could feel the rigid tension of his back as she clung to him. Obviously he was reacting in a typical male fashion. He'd been worried about her and now that it was clear that there was nothing wrong with her, he was angry. There was no logic to it, of course, but she doubted if he'd appreciate her pointing that out.

She'd meant it when she said that she was sorry she'd worried him, but to herself she admitted that she was glad he cared enough to *be* worried. It wasn't a declaration of love, but it was a start in the right direction.

Conner continued the silent treatment, even after he'd chosen a place for their small camp. He built a fire and rolled out the sleeping bag. When he silently handed her a plastic bag of trail mix, Laura's patience started to fray. It wasn't as if she'd committed a major crime.

"Are you going to ignore me for the rest of the night?" she asked.

Conner had been sitting on his heels next to the fire, carefully feeding it a few small branches. The heat disappeared with the sun and they were high enough for the nights to be uncomfortably chilly, even later in the summer. The only sign that he gave that he'd heard her was a slight stiffening of his shoulders.

Laura ate a handful of trail mix, though it tasted like dust in her mouth. "I suppose you think I had no business taking Missy out alone."

"I think the fact that she's snug in the barn and we're out here pretty much speaks for itself," he said after a moment. He stood up and dusted his hands together.

Laura flushed but angled her chin a little higher. "I dropped the reins on the ground just the way you always do."

"She isn't trained for ground hitching," he said evenly.

"Well, I didn't know that. When I saw she'd gone, I started to walk home. I'm sorry if you were worried," she said again. "But as you can see, I'm fine."

She gasped as Conner's hands shot out, catching her upper arms and dragging her to her feet. The light from the fire barely reached his face, leaving it all shadows and angles, his pale eyes glittering furiously down at her.

"I thought something had happened to you, damn it! I thought you'd been thrown. You could have been dead, for all I knew.'' There was anger in his voice but there was something else, an underlying fear.

She stared up at him, her thoughts scrambled, unable to put together a single sentence. From the look in his eyes, she knew he would have liked to shake her till her teeth rattled. She also knew he wouldn't do anything of the kind. But the emotions roiling inside him clearly demanded some kind of release. She was half expecting it when he dragged her up against his body, his mouth coming down on hers with powerful force.

Conner hadn't known what he was going to do until he felt her mouth under his. It wasn't anger that drove him, though anger certainly played a part. It was a fierce need to confirm that she was safe, that she was his, as if by claiming her as his own, he could rid himself of the fear that he might have lost her.

Laura opened her mouth to him, her hands coming up to rest against his chest. She tasted the need in him, though she wasn't sure of its source. But it didn't matter. She loved him. He needed her. For the moment, it was enough.

It was the way it so often was between them, hunger driving them, making them impatient with buttons and zippers. Conner needed to be inside her, needed it on some deep, primal level, as if only by joining their bodies could he be sure that she was safe.

Laura felt cool air against her legs as he jerked her jeans down and off, and she had a moment to be grateful that she'd already removed her boots. Her fingers struggled with the buttons on his shirt. He simply shoved hers up under her arms. She heard a sharp snap as the front clasp on her bra broke beneath his impatient hands and then his palms were on her breasts, molding and kneading the soft flesh, his callused thumbs rasping over her nipples.

Her knees weakened and her fingers lost all coordination. She curled her hands in to the fabric of his shirt, her head tilted back to allow him to plunder her mouth, her breasts thrusting into his hands.

Conner felt her surrender, down to the soles of his feet. He had to have her. Now. He lowered her to the sleeping bag, kneeling between her open thighs as he worked the buttons on his jeans. He wrenched his jeans open and shoved them down over his hips, releasing the swollen length of his arousal. He hadn't had her foresight and the thought of wrestling with his boots now had him cursing under his breath. But he would have held onto his control long enough to do it if she hadn't closed one small hand around him. Conner shuddered as her fingers slid down his rigid length to cup the heavy sac at its base.

"Please." Just that one word, breathed so softly that it might have been his imagination. But it wasn't his imagination that she was drawing him closer, urging him to complete their union.

"To hell with the damn boots," he muttered and lowered himself to her. He caught both her hands in one of his, linking his fingers over her slender wrists and drawing them over her head to press them against the fabric of the sleeping bag.

He entered her with one swift thrust, burying his aching flesh in her welcoming sheath, feeling the delicate ripples as her body stretched to accommodate him. Her hips arched, taking him deeper still and Conner groaned, knowing he couldn't last very long.

Laura cried out with pleasure as he bent to catch one pebbled nipple in his mouth, scoring the tender flesh between his teeth and then soothing it with his tongue. And all the while, his hips kept up a driving rhythm. She tugged at her hands, needing to hold him, but he refused to release her. When she cursed, he laughed, a purely masculine sound of triumph.

She would have demanded that he let her go, but her breath was suddenly stolen as a powerful climax swept over her. She arched wildly beneath him. And had her revenge when her body tightened over his, dragging him with her. He stiffened, his face going taut and hard in the firelight as she felt the powerful throbbing of his release inside her.

It was a long time before either of them had the breath to move or speak. Conner had loosened his hold on her wrists sometime during the endless waves of pleasure, and Laura slid her fingers into his hair, enjoying its silky feel.

There'd been something different about tonight, an emotional edge that she'd never felt before. Conner had given more of himself than he ever had. In more ways than one, she thought, wondering if it had occurred to him that he hadn't used protection. There was no reason to mention it now. What was done was done, and she didn't want anything to spoil the moment.

"I love you." She hadn't realized what she was going to say until the words left her mouth. But she wouldn't have taken them back, even if it had been possible. "I love you, Conner."

She felt him go still against her. The silence stretched, and she felt her heart break just a little when he couldn't give her the words she longed to hear in return, though she hadn't expected them.

He lifted his head, his eyes pale in the firelight. If there was something to read in his expression, the flickering light concealed it from her. But when he lifted one hand and threaded his fingers through her hair, there was no mistaking the tenderness in his touch.

"Laura."

He said nothing else, only her name, his voice achingly gentle, his hand trembling against her jaw as he lowered his mouth to hers. It was enough for now, she thought, holding him. He'd accepted her love and that was more than he would have done a few short weeks ago.

She moaned softly beneath his mouth as she felt him swelling inside her. It was not as urgent this time but longer, slower and somehow even more intense, though that hardly seemed possible. She arched beneath him at last, clinging to him as the universe rocked around them. And only the stars heard their cries.

Chapter 11

There was a change in their relationship after that night. When Conner brought her home the next morning, the walls he'd built around himself were weaker than they had been when he went to find her.

They'd slept in each other's arms, waking to make love again as the sun rose. At her climax, she'd cried out that she loved him and Conner had shuddered against her, feeling the words shower over him like a benediction, soothing some secret ache in his soul.

They'd breakfasted on granola and a handful of dried fruit, while the sun edged its way above the horizon. It was the most beautiful dawn they'd ever seen. There was little conversation during the ride home. Conner was vividly aware of Laura's arms around his waist, of the soft pressure of her breasts against his back.

I love you, Conner. The words echoed in his mind, nagged at his thoughts.

He hadn't asked her to love him, he thought uneasily. That hadn't been part of the bargain when they'd married. He'd certainly never suggested that love had anything to do with their arrangement. Yet here she was, saying she loved him, seeming to ask nothing in return. She'd made a gift of her feelings, giving it to him without ties. And God help him, but he found himself wanting to hear the words again, wanting to see the look in her eyes when she said them.

It was an uncomfortable realization, one he was afraid to examine too closely. Why should he want to hear how she felt when he couldn't—wouldn't—return those feelings. That part of him had been buried three years ago and the odd stirrings he felt when he looked at Laura had nothing to do with love. He couldn't deny the nearly insatiable physical hunger he felt for her, but that didn't mean he loved her. He refused to love her.

It was still early when they rode into the ranch yard, and they had not yet reached the barn when the front door of the house opened and Mary came tumbling down the steps.

"'Aura! 'Aura!"

Conner reached back and took Laura's arm, swinging her to the ground in time to catch the pajama-clad bundle hurtling across the yard. She caught the little girl up in her arms, burying her face in Mary's hair, holding her close. He lifted his hand to Gun, who leaned against one of the posts that framed the porch, watching the reunion.

Well, that was one thing that had turned out just as he'd planned, Conner thought as he swung down off the horse. He'd told himself he was marrying Laura for Mary's sake and there was no doubt that the ties between the two of them were strong and solid.

Mary was talking a mile a minute, apparently feeling that Laura needed to be caught up on every single thing that had happened while she was away. Conner's smile had a rueful twist as he led the gray into the barn for a well-deserved rubdown and some grain. It was too bad that life wasn't as simple as it seemed at Mary's age. Love could be freely accepted and just as freely given. There was no questioning the right or wrong of it, no worrying about the price that might be exacted somewhere down the line.

He only wished he could view it the way a three-year-old did.

Though his response had not been that of her dreams, Laura felt no regret at having told Conner that she loved him. The time had felt right. She hadn't been able to hold it inside another minute. Hadn't someone once said that love wasn't really love unless it was freely given? She'd given her love, freely, without regret and without expectation. Which was just as well, she acknowledged ruefully, because Conner hadn't exactly jumped at the opportunity to tell her that he loved her, too.

But the words had meant something to him. In that moment they'd been too closely linked, in every way, for her to mistake his reaction. She sensed a conflict in him, as if he were torn between past and present, between the memory of what he'd lost and the fear of risking that kind of hurt again.

For the moment, it was enough that there *was* a conflict. As far as she was concerned, they had their whole lives in front of them. She could be patient. They had plenty of time.

The summer drifted by, one sunny day following the next. Conner's worries about the possibility of drought proved unfounded. Enough rain fell to keep the grass growing as well as to irrigate Laura's garden.

The day she picked her first tomato, she served it at dinner, carefully cutting it into four wedges and presenting it as if it were a truffle flown via the Concorde straight from the woods of France. Mary popped her section in her mouth and devoured it without ceremony, but Gun and Conner had a deeper understanding of the importance of the moment.

"The aroma is full-bodied, don't you think?" That was Gun, holding the tomato wedge between his fingers and inhaling the scent.

"Piquant, with just a touch of acid," Conner said, nodding solemnly. He bit into the tomato and chewed slowly. "Definitely a superior vintage. Modest, with just a trace of impertinence to give it some bounce."

"I'm going to give you some bounce," Laura threatened. "Just tell me it's a great tomato."

"It's a great tomato," both men said in unison.

"Pearls before swine," she huffed.

"'Mato.'' Mary reached out and took the tomato wedge from Laura's plate and popped it in her mouth, chewing with every evidence of pleasure. "Good."

She seemed bewildered by the laughter of the adults.

There was plenty of work, but there was also time for a few lazy summer afternoons. They spent the Fourth of July at the Williamses', where Cy prepared what he modestly claimed was the best barbecued beef in the world. Laura couldn't dispute the title. It was the best she'd ever eaten.

Watching Conner pitch horseshoes and Mary splashing in the wading pool that had been set up for the children, Laura felt a sense of belonging. Los Angeles was a thousand miles and a million lifetimes away. This was her home now, her life was here. She had a husband, a child and friends. And given time, she felt sure she'd have the love she craved.

Laura would have been content to let things drift along as they were indefinitely. Conner was changing. She could feel it. There was a tenderness in the way he made love to her, an emotional hunger that went even deeper than the undeniable physical hunger that burned hot as ever between them.

Given time, she was sure he'd find a way to let go of the past completely and look to the future, one they could share without ghosts.

She might have been content to let things go on as they were, but fate had a different idea. Summer began to wind down. Though the temperature remained warm, the days were shorter. In a few weeks the days would be cooler and the aspen leaves would start to change, painting the canyons with a hundred shades of gold.

For Laura, who'd grown up in Southern California, where autumn was more a concept than a reality, there was a gentle melancholy to the season, a feeling that something was coming to an end. But before she could become too absorbed in it, she realized that a new and more personal change had taken place.

She was pregnant.

The suspicion had been niggling at the back of her mind for a little while, but it wasn't until she made a trip to town and bought a little pink-and-blue box that she allowed the suspicion to surface. Taking care to wait until Conner had left for the day, she followed the instructions on the box and held her breath while she watched for the change.

Though she'd been expecting it, when she saw the color change, she felt almost faint with shock. It was confirmed. She was going to have a baby.

Staring at her reflection in the mirror, she sought some outward sign of the changes that were taking place in her body, but there was nothing she could see. If it was true that pregnant women had a glow about them, she couldn't see it in herself. At least not yet.

It must have happened that night when Conner had found her after her horse came home without her. She'd thought about the possibility at the time, but then she'd managed to put it from her thoughts. And Conner had never mentioned the risk they'd taken. Was it possible that he hadn't thought about it?

Conner. How was he going to react to this news? Would he be upset? She chewed on her lower lip.

They'd never talked about having children. It had seemed like one of those things that could be discussed "someday."

They'd only been married a few months. She had barely accustomed herself to being a wife and mother. Though she'd thought she'd like to have another child, she'd been in no rush. There was lots of time left on her biological clock. Now "someday" was here and she hadn't the faintest idea how her husband felt about becoming a father again.

No, that wasn't quite true. She might not have talked to him about it, but she thought she had a pretty good idea of his feelings. He'd only just begun to make a connection with the daughter he already had. His relationship with Mary had improved a great deal over the past few weeks. But it had taken him over three years to get to that point.

But Mary's mother died having her. In his grief, he'd set up barriers and no one had been there to help him tear them down. It wasn't really Mary he'd been shutting out; it was the pain of losing her mother.

But he'd loved Rachel, she thought bleakly. And he'd still closed himself off from her child.

She flattened her palm over her still-flat stomach, as if to reassure the tiny life she carried. It would be all right, she told herself. She'd choose her time carefully and tell him the news. Once he was over the initial shock, he'd . . .

He'd what? The truth was that she just didn't know. In so many ways, he remained an enigma to her.

* * *

She still didn't know a week later. She told herself that it was important to choose the right time and that it just hadn't appeared yet. In her more honest moments, she knew she was putting off telling him because she was afraid to upset the fragile balance they'd found. It might not be a perfect marriage, but they'd made progress. Now everything was going to change, and she wasn't sure that change would be for the better.

If Conner noticed that she seemed a little distracted, he didn't mention it, though she caught him looking at her once or twice, his eyes questioning. She almost wished he would ask her what was wrong. Maybe then she'd find the courage to get the words out, to tell him that they were going to be parents before next spring.

But the days slipped by and she kept her secret, holding it close to her heart, rejoicing over it in private even as she worried about the results of revealing it to the one person who had as much right to know as she did.

She'd known about her pregnancy for almost two weeks and she knew she couldn't put off the moment of truth much longer. For one thing, she really ought to see a doctor. Though she didn't need the pregnancy confirmed and she'd never felt better physically in her life, she knew she'd feel better having a professional tell her that everything was going just as it should.

And the night before, Conner had commented on how sensitive her breasts were. She'd felt her heart stop, wondering if he would make the connection, half hoping he would so that the waiting and wondering would be over at last. But he hadn't, and the secret was still hers alone. But not for long, she promised herself. She'd tell him tonight, no matter what.

As it happened, he found out sooner than that, but not in any way she'd planned. She had, in the months since she'd started learning to ride, never been thrown. In her more pragmatic moments, she guessed that the reason for this had as much to do with the mounts Conner provided for her than with any particular skill. But she liked to think that it was at least in some part her own doing that kept her in the saddle.

On this particular afternoon, she had planned to ride only to the end of their private road to pick up the mail. It was a task that Conner was inclined to let go for two or three days, pointing out, with undeniable logic, that he wasn't expecting anything that couldn't wait to be fetched. Laura found this attitude amazing since, to her, mailboxes were more like treasure chests than anything else. You simply never knew what wonders might await, anything from a catalog for things you'd never known you wanted to an offer to participate in a sweepstakes for unheard-of riches.

Since she almost, literally, could not sleep at night for thinking about what might be languishing in the mailbox, she'd made a habit to pick up the mail herself. Usually she drove the mile and a half to the road, but today she felt the need for a little reflective time so she decided to ride.

Gun saddled Missy for her and as soon as Laura swung up on the mare's back, Mary immediately clamored to "ride hosey, too." Laughing, Laura nodded for Gun to hand the little girl up to her. She shifted back in the saddle as Gun lifted Mary up. Maybe it was the combination of feeling Laura's weight shift and catching a glimpse of Mary's bright pink overalls from the corner of her eye. Maybe a bee stung her. But whatever it was, Missy, who was usually the most placid of animals, shied violently away from Gun.

Laura had been more concerned with getting Mary settled than she had been with maintaining her seat, and she failed to move with her mount. The reins slid from her hand as the mare went one way and she went the other. There was a split-second awareness that she was falling and then the ground slammed into her. It wasn't a bad fall, really. She'd merely tumbled from the horse, not been thrown from it. But she hit the ground with enough force to knock the air from her lungs.

For several seconds, all she saw was a gray haze. Her chest felt tight and she felt panic hovering at the edges of her thoughts. With a gasp, she sucked air back into her aching lungs. She blinked and her vision began to clear. Gun and Conner knelt on either side of her, their faces tight with concern. She could hear Mary crying, but she had a more pressing concern than the little girl's tears.

Her breath catching on a frightened sob, she flattened her fingers over her stomach and blurted out the only words she could think of.

"The baby."

Conner reared back as if he'd been struck, the color draining from his face. He opened his mouth, but not a word came out. Gun threw him a quick look. Assessing the shock on his friend's face, it wasn't hard to guess that this was the first Conner had heard of a baby.

"I'm sure he's fine," Gun said, when it seemed as if Conner was struck speechless. He set his hand over Laura's. "Probably doesn't even know his mother took a tumble. They're a lot tougher than you think."

Laura didn't even think to question what he knew about babies. She clung to the reassurance in his voice, needing to believe he was right.

"Everything feel all right?" Gun asked.

"I think so." Now that she was over the initial shock, she took a quick inventory and decided that everything seemed to be in working order. "Help me sit up."

Though he'd yet to say a word, it was Conner's arm that slid under her and helped her ease to a sitting position. Laura stole a quick look at his face, vividly aware that her announcement hadn't been made in quite the way she'd planned. But if he felt any emotion at learning that he was to become a father again, she couldn't see any signs of it. His features were controlled and without expression, his light green eyes revealing nothing of what he was thinking or feeling.

With a sigh that hovered on the edge of tears, she turned from him and opened her arms to Mary, who stood trembling and frightened in the curve of Gun's arm. The little girl rushed to her, burrowing her small body into Laura's, tiny arms locking around her neck in a near stranglehold.

"It's all right," she said, patting Mary's back. She only wished she were sure that it was the truth.

"You should lie down." Conner spoke for the first time since she'd inadvertently dropped her bomb. No matter how much she wanted to, Laura couldn't read anything more than impersonal concern, either in his words or in his expression.

Feeling as fragile as a china doll, she let him help her to her feet, though Gun had to pry Mary loose before that could be accomplished. Once standing, Laura found that she was shakier than she would have believed. She didn't know whether it was a result of the fall or a result of the emotional uncertainty she felt.

But after a moment, her knees regained their strength and she was able to straighten away from Conner's support. Mary continued to cry, perhaps sensing the tension among the adults and thinking it was caused by Laura's fall.

"Here. Give her to me." She held out her arms for Mary, but Conner was there first.

"I'll take her," he said shortly. Mary clung to Gun for a moment before consenting to go to her father. With an encouraging smile in Laura's direction, Gun went to pick up the mare's reins to lead her back into the barn.

Laura thought of the old rule about getting right back up when you were thrown off a horse, but she had no intention of climbing back into the saddle right away. In fact, she wasn't sure she'd be doing any riding for the next seven months or so. Thinking of the fear she'd felt, she flattened her hand over her stomach in an unconscious gesture of protection.

She'd given so much thought to how Conner was going to react to the news that she was pregnant, that she hadn't taken much time to consider how *she* really felt. It wasn't until she'd thought there might be some danger of losing it that she'd realized how much she wanted this baby.

She was so caught up in the realization that she missed the look Conner threw her and the way his eyes darkened when he saw the revealing position of her hand.

Mary had stopped crying by the time they reached the porch, though her breath continued to come in shaken little aftersobs. She lay against Conner's shoulder, tired out by the emotional storm.

"I think she should go down for a nap," Laura said.

"I think you should both lie down." Conner carried his daughter into the master bedroom and set her on the big bed. "You both need a rest."

She would have been touched by his concern if it hadn't been delivered in such an impersonal tone. As if she were a guest whose well-being was his responsibility. He saw Mary settled against the pillows and then turned toward the door.

"Conner." Laura caught his arm, afraid that he might not stop if she didn't actually physically hold him. "We need to talk."

"Not now." His eyes skimmed over her face, but she wasn't sure he really saw her. "We'll talk later."

She might have argued if it hadn't been for Mary's plaintive cry from the bed. "'Aura." Her voice hovered on the edge of fresh tears. With a sigh, Laura dropped her hand from Conner's arm.

"Later," she agreed.

Their talk, which occurred later that night and only because Laura stayed up until Conner came to bed, was short and unsatisfactory.

"There's not that much to discuss," Conner said, tugging his shirt off tiredly. "Are you feeling all right?"

"Yes. I haven't had any morning sickness or anything. At least not yet." She sat up in bed, drawing her knees up and linking her arms around them.

"Good. Have you seen a doctor?"

"No."

"You should make an appointment." He sat down on the edge of the bed to tug his boots off.

Laura stared at his back in frustration. This wasn't going at all the way she'd planned. He was too calm, too cool. He'd retreated behind those walls again, determined to reveal nothing of what he was feeling or thinking.

"I was going to tell you about it tonight."

"Were you?" He set his boots on the floor and unsnapped his jeans.

"Yes." Her teeth worried at her lower lip. "Don't you want to ask questions or yell or something?"

That brought his eyes to her, but they were flat and unreadable. "I don't think I have any questions. You're pregnant. I assume you got that way the night we camped out. We took a stupid chance and got caught." He shrugged, apparently not seeing her wince

at his harsh dismissal of a night that had seemed close
to paradise to her. "And I can't think of any reason to
yell. What's done is done. The fault was mine. I'd
have to be an even bigger SOB than I am to shout at
you over it."

Laura was silent as he finished undressing and got
into bed. Without another word, he reached out to
turn off the lamp on his side of the bed. There was
something very final in that small click. After a moment, she did the same on her side, then slid back
down under the covers.

On the surface, everything seemed fine. He'd taken
the news well. Too well, in fact. She didn't want to see
this calm control. She wanted him to tell her what he
was thinking, what he was feeling. Was he angry? Did
her pregnancy bring back memories of Rachel's, of
losing her? Was he worried that the same thing might
happen to her? Did he care enough to worry? It was a
long time before she fell asleep.

Conner lay awake until almost dawn, staring into
the darkness, haunted by memories he'd almost managed to escape. When he finally did fall asleep, his
sleep was disturbed by images of Laura, her stomach
heavy with the weight of his child, her eyes smiling at
him. Only then she wasn't smiling anymore and there
was blood, so much blood and she'd turned her face
away. He reached out to turn her back toward him,
but it wasn't Laura's face anymore. It was Rachel's,
still and cold, all the life drained from her. Then it was
Laura lying there, her blue eyes closed forever.

And the knowledge that he was alone again crashed
over him, suffocating him with the weight of his own

loneliness. He woke suddenly, his heart pounding, his skin cold and clammy with sweat.

Careful not to disturb Laura, Conner slid out of bed and went to the window, pushing aside the drapes to stare out into the gray predawn light. He couldn't go through it again. Bracing his arms on the windowsill, he leaned his forehead against the cold glass.

It was only a nightmare, he told himself.

Nightmare? Or was it some kind of premonition, a knowledge that history was going to repeat itself?

He had no answer for that.

For nearly a week, Laura nudged at the wall he'd put up. She tried to get him to talk to her about how he felt about her unexpected pregnancy. But his answer was always the same. It was a fact. What was there to discuss? There was plenty to discuss, if only she could get him to admit it.

All the progress she'd thought they'd made seemed as ephemeral as a morning fog that vanished at the first touch of the sun's heat. Didn't he understand that you couldn't work your way through a problem as long as you refused to admit it existed? Or did their marriage mean so little to him that he didn't care whether they worked their way through this or not? Had she been lying to herself, thinking that she'd managed to edge her way partway through those damned walls of his? Had it all just been one of her fantasies?

It was thoughts like these that led her to seek out the comfort of the barn. Mary had gone to Cy and Dottie's for one last day with The Horde before the visi-

tors scattered in several directions to return home
before the school year began. The house seemed to
echo with emptiness, though Laura knew it was an
emptiness she carried inside herself.

She liked the barn. It was full of warm animal smells
and the soft rustlings of the occupants. Several of the
horses thrust their heads over the top of their stall
doors to greet her. She scratched behind their ears,
feeling warmed by their uncomplicated company. She
didn't have to worry about whether any of them were
concealing their thoughts from her.

When she reached Missy's stall, she let herself inside, presenting the mare with the sugar cube she'd
brought for the purpose. They'd made their peace the
day after Laura took her fall. Laura fancied the mare
was embarrassed about losing her rider and she'd reassured her that there were no hard feelings. In seven
months or so, she'd be willing to resume their rides,
but in the meantime, she simply enjoyed the mare's
companionship.

Having crunched the sugar cube between her strong
teeth, Missy indicated a willingness to have her neck
rubbed. She butted her head against Laura's shoulder, snorting her pleasure. Laura smiled and then felt
the smile waver as tears filled her eyes.

"Oh, Missy, what am I going to do?" The mare
snorted and bobbed her head, and Laura found herself with her face buried in her coarse mane, her
shoulders shaking with sobs.

She didn't know how long she'd been crying when
she felt strong hands close over her shoulders, turn-

ing her away from the horse. Gun was hardly more than a large, blurry shadow through her tears.

"I think you'll find my shoulder a bit more comfortable to cry on," he offered lightly.

"I'm not crying." The absurd denial made perfect sense to her.

"Good." He pressed one large hand between her shoulder blades and urged her forward. "Why don't you not cry until you feel better?"

Laura clung to his shirtfront, sniffling and sobbing. She hadn't cried at all this past week. No matter how frustrated and scared she'd been by the way Conner had closed himself away from her, she hadn't given in to tears. But once started, the flood seemed never ending.

Gun didn't offer any soothing platitudes and he didn't seem to expect an explanation for the tears she wasn't crying. He simply held her and let her cry out all her hurt and anger until the sobs finally died down to hiccuping breaths. Still without speaking, he fished a handkerchief out of his back pocket and offered it to her.

"Thank you." Leaning against him like a tired child, Laura wiped her eyes and blew her nose. She felt completely drained. "You're a good friend," she said finally, looking up at him.

"Damn right I am. I don't let just anybody act like a watering pot all over my favorite shirt." His words drew a faint smile from her and he reached up to brush his thumb roughly over her cheek. "Anytime you need a shoulder, you're welcome to come find me."

"Thanks, but I don't often . . ."

"Get your hands off my wife." Conner's voice was low and hard.

"Conner!" Laura spun to face him, probably looking the picture of guilt, she realized immediately. Only she had nothing to feel guilty about. She lifted her chin.

"Calm down, Conner. Laura was just a little upset." Gun's voice was calm, but it held an underlying note of steel that said his temper wasn't as deeply buried as it might have been.

"You don't owe anybody an explanation, Gun," Laura snapped. She might as well have not spoken for all the attention they paid her.

"It's not your job to comfort her when she's upset," Conner said tightly. "She's my wife."

"And it's about time you realized it," Gun said, stepping forward. At some point while she was crying, he'd moved them out of Missy's stall, and the two men now faced each other in the wide pathway between the stalls.

"Butt out, Larsen." Conner's hands were clenched into fists at his side, his eyes glittering with rage.

"No, damn it, I won't butt out. You're right. She shouldn't have been crying on my shoulder. She shouldn't need to cry on *anyone's* shoulder. Only you're too damned stupid to see the nose on your face."

"Gun . . ."

"No, it's got to be said. And I'm just mad enough to say it." He shrugged off Laura's attempt to quiet him and continued to glare at Conner. "You're too busy living in the past to know what a lucky bastard you are right here in the present. Do you really think this is what Rachel would have wanted? You hanging her memory around your neck like a dead albatross?''

Conner moved with lightning speed, his right fist coming up and connecting solidly with Gun's jaw. Gun staggered back and then caught himself. With a sound remarkably close to a growl, he launched himself on Conner and the two of them hit the ground.

Laura's pleas for sanity went unheard, as did her increasingly angry demands that they stop. When she saw that words weren't going to get through to them, she looked around for a more effective means of communication. She found it in the water hose looped over a hook. Grabbing the nozzle, she turned the faucet handle on as far as it would go and turned the spray on the two men, who were still rolling on the floor, apparently attempting to kill each other.

Finding themselves suddenly drenched, they broke apart, rolling to a sitting position and cursing as the full force of the spray hit them squarely in the face. Only when she was satisfied that she had their full attention did Laura turn the water off. As the spray died down to a trickle and then a slow drip, the barn suddenly seemed unnaturally quiet. Conner and Gun stared at her, and she glared back at them.

She racked her brain for words scathing enough to convey her opinion of their actions. When nothing came to her, she settled for the one unanswerable accusation.

"Men!" She packed the single syllable with so much contempt that they both winced. With a last furious look in their direction, she turned and stalked out of the barn, her back rigid with anger. The two men stared after her in silence.

"You've got one hell of a woman there," Gun said finally.

"I know."

"Then why don't you tell her as much?"

"Why don't you mind your own damned business?" Conner snapped, climbing to his feet.

"You're right." Gun nodded and accepted the hand Conner held down to pull him to his feet. "It's about time I was moving on. Somewhere south, I think. I've stayed longer than I'd intended."

"You're always welcome." Conner dabbed at his split lip.

"I appreciate that." Gun shifted his jaw carefully, checking to make sure it was in working order.

They shook hands, in perfect accord with one another.

If Laura had been there, there wouldn't have been a word strong enough to express her disgust at such male behavior.

Her anger had carried her as far as the kitchen, where she began getting out the ingredients for bread. Maybe a few minutes spent pummeling a mound of dough would improve her mood, though she'd rather have been pummeling something more satisfying—like her husband's stubborn head.

She heard Conner come in, but she didn't turn to look at him. She scooped flour out of the canister and measured it into a bowl, counting the cups as if she had nothing else on her mind.

"Laura?" She felt an almost feral pleasure in the cautious way he spoke her name.

"What?"

"I'm sorry. I acted like an idiot."

"Yes, you did." But there was no anger in her agreement. There was nothing more disarming than a sincere apology.

"Do you have a minute?"

"Not really." She'd thought she'd cried out every tear in her body, yet she felt the backs of her eyes sting anew at the sound of his voice. "I need to get this bread going," she said, as if the fate of nations depended on this loaf of bread.

"I owe you an apology for more than today," Conner said, determined to get the words out. He must have crossed the kitchen because his voice came from directly behind her. How did he manage to move so quietly in boots, she wondered, focusing on the question to avoid acknowledging the tentative flicker of hope his words brought to life inside her.

"Gun was right in some ways." She could hear what the words cost him and she forced herself to turn and look up at him.

"What was Gun right about?"

"About my holding on to the past. About not seeing the nose on my face," he admitted with a half smile that held more pain than humor.

"No one expects you to forget the past."

"Maybe it's time I did just that. Rachel would have been the first to say so."

It was the first time he'd deliberately brought up Rachel's name, and Laura felt the hope grow a little bit.

"When she died, a big part of me died with her," he continued. "I didn't know it was possible to hurt that much and still be alive. I swore I'd never risk that kind of hurt again."

"Gun told me she died when Mary was born," Laura said, deciding that she'd better take advantage of his willingness to talk since there was no way of knowing whether or not it would last.

"Gun seems to have poked his nose into a lot of things he shouldn't have," Conner said, frowning.

"I asked him about . . . Rachel. When you wouldn't talk about her, I asked him what she was like. She sounded like someone I'd have liked." And she hoped he couldn't see how much that admission had cost her.

"I think she'd have liked you, too," he said, looking at her thoughtfully. He reached out and caught one of her hands in his, rubbing his thumb absentmindedly across her palm.

"Just because Rachel died in childbirth doesn't mean I'm going to." She rushed the words out before she could change her mind. The restless movement stopped and his fingers tightened almost painfully around hers. Laura wondered if she'd gone too far.

"I don't think I could survive another loss like that," he said hoarsely. The skin seemed too tight over his cheekbones, giving his face a stark look.

"You won't have to." Laura brought her fingers up to soothe away the lines of tension that bracketed his mouth. Inside, she felt the hope become a steady flame. Did he realize that he'd just admitted that he cared for her, that he didn't want to lose her? "I'm young and healthy and there's not a reason in the world why anything should go wrong."

There hadn't been any reason for anything to go wrong with Rachel, either, he thought bleakly. But he didn't say the words out loud.

"If you can forgive me for being such a jerk lately, I'll try to clean up my act," he said instead, forcing a smile he didn't really feel.

All he could think of was that she was carrying his child. The last woman who'd carried his child had died. She was right, of course. There wasn't a chance in a million that anything would go wrong this time. But logic was a poor argument against the gut-deep fear lodged inside him.

"I love you, Conner." Laura's smile was soft and gentle. "A few days of you being a jerk isn't enough to make me change my mind about that."

He slid his arms around her and drew her close, as much to hide his bleak expression from her as to feel her warmth against him. Rachel had loved him, too.

And that love had killed her.

Chapter 12

Laura's first real autumn was a time of change, some good, some sad. Gun left, and she missed him more than she'd expected. When Conner told her he was leaving, she'd been afraid that it was because of the fight the two of them had had. But with an attitude that could only make sense to a man, he'd shrugged the fight off as being unimportant. She didn't quite believe him until she talked to Gun.

"We've known each other too long to let a little rough-and-tumble cause a problem." Gun grinned at her and continued packing.

"Then why are you leaving?"

"It's time. I've been here long enough."

"We'll miss you."

"I'll miss you, too." His smile slipped a little, allowing a glimpse of old sorrows. "Have patience with

Conner, Laura. He loves you. He's just too stupid to see it.''

''I hope you're right.'' Laura blinked back tears and smiled at him. ''I can be pretty stubborn when I want to be. Besides, I've got a good reason to be patient.'' She smoothed one hand over her flat stomach.

''One of these days Conner will realize how lucky he is—having you and Mary and this place to call home.'' Gun's smile was twisted.

Laura wondered what was in his past that gave his eyes such a haunted look. She didn't ask, knowing he'd only laugh off the question. She had the feeling that Gun was looking for something, or someone. Whoever, or whatever it was, she hoped he'd find it and that it would drive the shadows from his eyes.

Gun left the next day, and his departure left a sore spot in her heart. Mary missed him, too, asking repeatedly when Unca Gun was coming back. Laura hoped she wasn't lying to her by saying that he'd be back.

The changes that occurred in her relationship with Conner were bittersweet. Certainly no one could have asked for a more tender lover. She'd missed sleeping in his arms, missed the sound of his heartbeat under her ear. She reveled in his touch, in the magic the two of them created together. But she craved the words of affection she knew he might never be able to give her.

He went with her when she visited the doctor and he was solicitous of her health, but she sensed the distance he kept between himself and the miracle she carried. As her stomach expanded, she sometimes saw him staring at it, his eyes brooding. It was as if he were

trying to look inside her, trying to predict the outcome of her pregnancy.

Laura's heart ached with love for him and for the
child she carried. And it ached for herself. She wanted
so much for him to be able to share her wonder at
what was happening. She wanted him to feel his baby
move within her and see his eyes light with joy.

Instead, she saw the haunted look in his eyes and
knew he was remembering another woman, another
pregnancy. No matter how much he struggled to conceal it, she knew what he was thinking. Knew also that
he felt none of her joy but only the fear that history
would repeat itself. No amount of reassurance, from
her or from the doctor, could soothe that fear.

Remembering Gun's words about having patience,
Laura told herself that once the baby was born and
Conner could see that his fears were unfounded, things
would change.

There were a few moments that gave her hope.
Watching Conner and Mary trudging through the
season's first snowfall to check on the animals, Mary's
tiny figure in its red snowsuit dwarfed by her father's,
her hand held securely in his. Laura pressed her cheek
against the cold glass and let her hand rest on the bulge
of her stomach, her eyes stinging with tears. He had
so much to give, if only he'd let himself.

"He'll love you once you're here," she said fiercely,
talking to the child she carried. "He loves you now.
He's just afraid to admit it."

A few nights later, she woke in the middle of the
night, coming out of some dream she couldn't quite
grab hold of but that had left her feeling warm and

content. As the size of her stomach had grown, her sleeping habits had changed. It was no longer comfortable for her to snuggle up against Conner's side, her head on his shoulder. They'd gradually settled on sleeping spoon fashion, her back against his chest, his legs drawn up under hers.

Tonight was no different. Still half asleep, she could feel the heat of Conner's chest along her back, the muscled strength of his legs against hers. She felt wonderfully safe and secure and loved, though he'd yet to say the words. She'd just begun to drift off again when she felt Conner's hand, which had been resting on her hip, move.

It took all her concentration to keep her breathing steady as his fingers settled ever so lightly over the swell of her stomach. His hand flattened over her so that he cradled the swollen mound that held his child. She felt the baby move inside her, as if greeting its father. Conner's fingers shifted gently to answer that small movement. There was something in the touch that made her think it wasn't the first time he'd held her this way.

She kept her breathing light and steady, not bothering to lift a hand to brush away the solitary tear that escaped.

Her first Christmas as Conner's wife was the most wonderful she'd ever know, despite the walls that still lay between them. There was a light snowfall on Christmas Eve, and Conner laughed indulgently at Laura's excitement over a real white Christmas. Christmas Day was to be spent with Cy and Dottie, but Christmas Eve was just the three of them. Mary spent most of the evening crouched in front of the tree, studying the various packages under it as if hoping to develop X-ray vision.

Since there was no doubt that the Williamses would go overboard on Christmas dinner, Laura had deliberately fixed a light supper. Afterward, the three of them exchanged the gifts they'd bought each other.

Laura was touched that Conner had thought to take Mary shopping to buy her a gift and she thanked the little girl profusely for the hideously ugly pink-and-green paperweight that she'd picked out. Conner's grin was wicked, but she had her revenge when he opened the present Mary had chosen for him. The kelly green tie with large purple-and-yellow squiggles was exactly what he'd wanted, he told his daughter, ignoring Laura's grin.

She'd given considerable thought to her gifts for Conner, finally settling on a volume of movie trivia and a butter-soft sweater in a shade of green that reflected his eyes. Conner's gifts to her were a book of poetry that she'd once mentioned wanting and a sapphire blue velvet robe. It was hopelessly impractical and would become even more so once the baby was born, but Laura had never owned anything more beautiful in her life.

"It reminded me of your eyes," Conner said, watching her snuggle her face against the plush fabric. Laura had to blink back tears.

But there was one last gift of the evening, one that no amount of money could have purchased. Mary had been absorbed in playing with the baby doll she'd been given, complete with a full wardrobe. Laura's motives had not been completely pure when she'd chosen the gift. She hoped that playing with the doll would help prepare Mary for the reality of having a real baby in the house.

The little girl had managed to remove the flannel nightie the doll had come in and was attempting to dress her in a pair of pink rompers. Success eluded her, and her small face scrunched with frustration. After a moment she stood up and brought the doll and the recalcitrant clothing over to where Laura sat on the sofa.

"Dress baby, Mama."

Laura's fingers closed around the doll even as she realized what Mary had just called her. She stared at her in shocked silence for a moment and then snatched her up and kissed her. Mary was willing to be kissed, but she was more interested in getting her doll clothed.

"Dress baby," she said again, pushing the doll into Laura's hands as if thinking she hadn't understood the request. "Mama dress."

"Mama'll dress," Laura promised. And she did, though her fingers were shaking and her eyes were blurred with tears. It wasn't until Mary had taken her doll and gone back to sit amidst the torn wrapping paper to play with it that Laura dared to look at Conner.

"Do you mind if she calls me that? I know I'm not really her mother—"

"Yes, you are." He reached out to take her hand, his smile bittersweet. "You're the only mother she's ever known."

"I don't want to try and take Rachel's place," she said, still hesitant about bringing up his first wife.

"You aren't. When she's older, we'll explain about Rachel." He slid one hand around her shoulder and drew her against his side, and Laura closed her eyes, savoring the closeness.

It wasn't often that he let his guard down like this, that he was willing to show her this side of himself. Someday it would always be like this, she promised herself. The three of them—four, she corrected, putting her hand on her stomach—would be a family. It was so easy to picture.

Conner would be sitting on the sofa. Mary would be beside him. Maybe he'd be reading her a story. Laura saw herself coming into the room, carrying a tiny newborn, and Conner immediately standing up and taking the baby from her, cradling it tenderly in his hands. He'd sit back down next to Mary, who'd peer at the blanket-wrapped bundle with just the right amount of older-sister affection.

It would happen that way, she thought. She was going to do everything she could to make sure it did.

By the middle of January, the light dusting of snow that had covered the ground since Christmas had disappeared, though the temperature stayed low. When Laura expressed her surprise that winter should be over so soon, Conner smiled and shook his head. The winter wasn't over, it was just being coy. The temperature might be a balmy fifty-five one day and then drop below zero the next. Laura had a difficult time imagining such unpredictable weather. In L.A. the weather reports could practically come on a monthly, rather than a daily basis.

The baby was due the middle of February, and she was feeling big and clumsy and anxious to hold her child in her arms. Conner had declared that she was going into town two weeks before her due date. The ranch was too isolated, the weather too unpredictable. He wasn't going to chance being snowed in with the baby due any minute.

It had been an order rather than a suggestion. Laura would have bristled over his tone if she hadn't seen the fear in his eyes. So she'd agreed to go stay at a hotel, even though she thought it unnecessary. It was only for a little while, she told herself. Once the baby was here and he saw that they were both all right, he'd see how wrong he'd been to worry.

As Conner had predicted it would, winter came back with a roar. He'd planned to drive Laura into town on a Thursday. On Monday, the temperature dropped and it began to snow. Not the soft, puffy little flakes Laura had admired at Christmas, but a wet, heavy snowfall that showed no signs of stopping. Tuesday, the sun shone with deceptive brilliance, sparkling on the new-fallen snow, seeming to apologize for yesterday's gray skies.

Conner seemed to relax a little, and she knew he'd been worried about being able to get her into town. She stroked her hand over the huge mound of her stomach and admitted to herself that maybe it wouldn't be such a bad idea to be closer to the hospital, after all. The quick shift in the weather had made her realize why Conner was so determined to have her off the ranch well before her labor began.

On Wednesday, it started to snow again. Conner looked at the sky, trying to judge how serious the weather might be. He was no closer to an answer when Dottie called and asked him if he could help them with the stock. Cy had broken his ankle when he slipped on a patch of ice a few days into the new year and he was worried about her trying to handle things on her own.

"Of course you have to go," Laura said when Conner told her about Dottie's call. "Mary and I will be fine here."

He gave the gray sky another uneasy look, but there was no way he could ignore the neighbor's request for help. His own stock was cared for. Laura saw him off, waving and smiling from the porch.

Her smile faded as she watched the truck slip and slide its way out of sight. Rubbing absently at the ache in her lower back, she looked up at the sky, wishing it were possible to read the clouds.

By the time Conner and Dottie had seen to the stock's needs, it was after dark. Snow began to drift down just as they rode into the yard. Conner sent Dottie up to the house while he cared for the horses. The smell of coffee and stew filled the house when he stepped into the kitchen, having stomped the snow off his boots on the back porch. He accepted the mug of coffee Cy handed him and reached for the phone to call Laura.

"We're fine," she told him a few moments later. "We're just getting ready to watch *The Wizard of Oz* for the four hundredth time this week.'' Mary never seemed to tire of the movie. She'd watched it so many times that Laura claimed she knew all the dialogue by heart.

''I don't like the idea of you trying to get home in the dark. The roads must be pretty icy. Why don't you stay there tonight?''

''No. I don't like you being there alone.''

''We're fine.''

They argued back and forth and when Dottie and Cy pitched in on Laura's side and urged him to stay the night, Conner reluctantly agreed. The roads were hell, but he still wasn't comfortable leaving her alone. She promised to call him no matter what the time if she needed anything.

The snow was still falling when he stretched out on the sofa. He'd stood at the window and watched it for a while, knowing how deceptive that slow, gentle-seeming fall could be. He finally lay down, but sleep proved elusive and he found himself dozing off and on. It was sometime after midnight when he started awake suddenly, sure that he'd heard the phone ring. He rolled off the sofa and stumbled toward the kitchen, cursing when he stubbed his toe on an end table he hadn't seen in the dark.

There'd been no repeat of the ring he thought he'd heard, but he picked the phone up anyway, expecting to hear a dial tone. But there was no dial tone, only the utter silence of a downed line. Conner stood there for several seconds, his fingers knotted over the receiver. Just because the phone was dead, it didn't mean that there was anything wrong. Phone lines went dead in storms. It was a given. But he couldn't get the sound of that ring out of his head. What if Laura had tried to call him and the line had gone down after just one ring?

What if she'd fallen and hurt herself or Mary had suddenly taken sick? Or, God forbid, what if the baby was coming early? He should have gone home earlier, he thought, groping his way back to the living room and flipping on a lamp there. He shouldn't have let her persuade him to stay the night. He pulled on his boots and found his coat and hat. Taking time only to scribble a quick note to let Cy and Dottie know he'd gone home, Conner let himself out into the night.

The temperature had dropped again and the snow was falling faster, piling up against the sides of the buildings, weighting the branches of the trees. The truck grumbled about starting but it finally cooperated; then Conner backed it around in the yard and pointed it in the general direction of the road.

The headlights reflected back off the swirling white curtain of snow. He could feel the tires fighting to get a grip on the icy road. He'd put on chains earlier, but even with that added traction, it was dicey.

His hands gripped the steering wheel with bruising force. His eyes ached with the strain of trying to see through the curtain of snow. He was as likely to end up in a ditch as he was to make it home. But he didn't slow down. He had to get home. There was something wrong. He knew it as surely as if he'd heard it on the news. Laura needed him. And he'd reach her or die trying.

A drive that normally took thirty minutes stretched to almost two hours. By the time Conner saw the bulk of the Rocking D barn loom up before the truck, his shoulders ached with tension and his jaw hurt from the pressure he'd been exerting on his clenched teeth. He shut the engine off and rested his forehead against the wheel for a moment, hardly able to believe that he'd made it in one piece.

When he pushed open the truck door, the cold rushed in at him, chilling him to the bone in seconds. Slamming the door, he ran toward the house, his movements made clumsy by the snow that promptly caked his boots. He shoved open the front door and staggered into the entryway, gasping in pain as the warm air hit his cold skin.

"Conner."

The sound of his name brought his head up. Laura leaned in the living room doorway, one hand pressed to the heavy mound of her stomach, the other clutching the doorjamb. She wore a flannel nightgown and her hair tumbled over her shoulders in a flurry of dark waves.

"Are you all right?" His voice was hoarse with strain as he stripped off his gloves and forced his cold fingers to work the buttons on his coat. Now that he was here, he felt no lessening of the urgency that had driven him out into the storm.

"The phone and electricity are out," she said. "Good thing the heater isn't electric. I started a fire in the fireplace and I boiled some water, but I don't know what to do with it."

"What the hell are you talking about?" He shrugged out of his coat and let it drop to the floor.

Laura's answer was not verbal. She gasped suddenly, her fingers digging into the wood of the doorjamb while her other hand clutched at her stomach. Conner felt as if he'd been kicked over the heart.

They were miles from town. No phone. No electricity. No way to call for help and no way for help to get to them even if they could call. It was snowing like it had no intention of stopping, and the roads were like polished glass to drive on. And she was in labor.

He reached her in two strides, sliding his arm around her shoulders as the contraction ended, letting her rest against him for a moment before he slipped his other arm under her knees and picked her up.

"I'm sorry," she whispered against his throat. "I know it's too soon. But it started about two hours ago. I tried to call you but the phone was already out. My water broke. And the bed's all wet." She started to cry as if a wet bed were the greatest of tragedies.

"Hush. It's all right." He stood in the middle of the living room, still holding her, and looked at the preparations she'd made. He found himself torn between laughter and tears. There were stacks of towels, enough to dry an elephant, at least. Every sheet in the house was piled in a heap next to the sofa. Three pans of water steamed on the hearth. There was string, scissors and a pile of newspapers from the utility room.

"Did you plan on reading the news?" he asked, surprised that he could find even a moment's humor in the situation.

"I saw it in a movie once," she admitted. "I think you're supposed to put the baby in them or something."

"Doris Day and James Garner," he said, picking his way through the piles of supplies and lowering her to the sofa.

"That's the one." She clutched at his hand when he started to straighten. "I was so scared, Conner. I was so afraid you'd come home and find everything had all gone wrong. And I was worried about Mary, what would happen if she woke up."

He felt something break loose inside him and he sank down next to her, pulling her into his arms. She'd been worried about him and about Mary.

"Nothing's going to go wrong," he said when he was sure he could control his voice.

She gasped and clutched at his hand as another contraction grabbed at her. Automatically he noted the time, thinking that it hadn't been very long since the last contraction. This was one first baby that didn't seem interested in taking its time arriving.

"I'm sorry," she said, when the contraction eased enough for her to speak. "I know how hard this is for you."

"Shut up." The command was so politely spoken that it took a moment for Laura to realize what he'd said. She lifted her head to stare at him in shock.

"You don't owe me any apologies. I'm the one who should apologize to you. I've been a selfish bastard all these months, letting old fears control me." His hand was not quite steady as he smoothed her hair back from her forehead. "I don't know why you didn't tell me to take a hike months ago."

"I love you," she said, as if that were the answer to everything. And maybe it was.

Conner looked into her eyes, seeing the purity of her love. He realized suddenly that the walls he'd built to protect himself had been prison walls, locking him away from life. He'd been safe, but he hadn't been alive.

"The smartest thing I ever did was walk into Rusty's Lounge that night," he said softly.

Laura's eyes widened at what she heard in his voice, what she saw in his gaze. Her heart started to beat more quickly and for a moment she forgot all about the baby.

"Conner?" There was hope as well as a question in her voice. Aching need and lingering fear in her eyes.

"I love you, Laura. Gun was right. I was just too big a fool to admit it until now."

"I love you, too. I—oh!" Another contraction cut her off in midword, but it didn't matter. There'd be time later to say all the things she'd been holding in her heart for so long.

A little less than three hours later, Conner delivered his son into the world. The baby was red-faced with temper and ready to let the world know that he'd arrived. Laughing and crying, Laura felt his sweet weight as Conner laid him on her breast where the baby would be able to feel the familiar rhythm of her heartbeat.

Conner's face was pale, his hands not quite steady as he tied string around the umbilical cord before cutting it. He couldn't believe it was over. There was bleeding, but it was normal, nothing like what had happened to Rachel. And Laura looked pale and exhausted, but her face sparkled with life. When she held out her hand to him, he took it and pressed it to his face, unashamed of the slow tears that dampened her fingers.

"I love you," she said, looking as if the sun were shining in her eyes.

"God, I love you, too," he said, his voice shaken.

The snow stopped before dawn and the clouds drifted away, leaving the sun to shine on the white landscape. Laura slept for a few hours, waking when she heard Conner cautioning Mary to be quiet. It seemed incredible that she'd slept through last night's events. Laura opened her eyes a crack and watched as Conner and Mary tiptoed across the room, stopping beside the sofa.

The baby slept in a dresser drawer lined with soft blankets. His face was still red and his nose was slightly flattened from the birthing process, but Laura could already see that he had his father's mouth and she had no doubt that those baby blue eyes would be the same cool green as Conner's one day.

"Did Santa come?" Mary whispered when she saw the baby.

"Not exactly." Conner glanced up and saw that Laura's eyes were open. "This was an altogether different miracle," he said softly.

"The very best kind," Laura whispered. "The kind made by love."

The kind that would last a lifetime.

* * * * *

NORA ROBERTS

Love has a language all its own, and for centuries flowers have symbolized love's finest expression. Discover the language of flowers—and love—in this romantic collection of 48 favorite books by bestselling author Nora Roberts.

Two titles are available every other month at your favorite retail outlet.

In June, look for:

One Summer, Volume #31
Gabriel's Angel, Volume #32

In August, look for:

The Name of the Game, Volume #33
A Will and a Way, Volume #34

Collect all 48 titles and become fluent in

THE LANGUAGE of LOVE

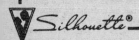

Silhouette®
™

OFFICIAL RULES • MILLION DOLLAR BIG WIN SWEEPSTAKES
NO PURCHASE OR OBLIGATION NECESSARY TO ENTER

MEN MADE IN AMERICA

Fifty red-blooded, white-hot, true-blue hunks from every
State in the Union!

Beginning in May, look for MEN MADE IN AMERICA!
Written by some of our most popular authors, these
stories feature fifty of the strongest, sexiest men, each
from a different state in the union!

Two titles available every other month at your favorite
retail outlet.

In July, look for:

CALL IT DESTINY by Jayne Ann Krentz (Arizona)
ANOTHER KIND OF LOVE by Mary Lynn Baxter
(Arkansas)

In September, look for:

DECEPTIONS by Annette Broadrick (California)
STORMWALKER by Dallas Schulze (Colorado)

You won't be able to resist MEN MADE IN AMERICA!

INTIMATE MOMENTS®

10TH

Anniversary

Celebrate our anniversary with a fabulous collection of firsts....

Silhouette Books is proud to present a FREE hardbound collection of the first Silhouette Intimate Moments® titles written by three of your favorite authors:

NIGHT MOVES
by *New York Times* best-selling author **Heather Graham Pozzessere**

LADY OF THE NIGHT
by **Emilie Richards**

A STRANGER'S SMILE
by **Kathleen Korbel**

This unique collection will not be available in retail stores and is only available through this exclusive offer.

INTIMATE MOMENTS®

10TH

Anniversary

ONE PROOF OF PURCHASE

082 KAR-R